D0461672

HALINKA

HALT

Mirjam Pressler

Translated from the German by
Elizabeth D. Crawford

INKA

Henry Holt and Company
New York

Henry Holt and Company, Inc., *Publishers since 1866*
115 West 18th Street, New York, New York 10011

Henry Holt is a registered trademark of Henry Holt and Company, Inc.

First published in the United States in 1998 by
Henry Holt and Company, Inc.
Published in Canada by Fitzhenry & Whiteside Ltd.,
195 Allstate Parkway, Markham, Ontario L3R 4T8.
Originally published in Germany in 1994 by
Beltz Verlag under the title *Wenn das Glück kommt
muss man ihm einen Stuhl hinstellen.*

Library of Congress Cataloging-in-Publication Data
Pressler, Mirjam.
[Wenn das Glück kommt muss man ihm einen Stuhl hinstellen. English]
Halinka / Mirjam Pressler; translated from the German by Elizabeth D. Crawford.
    p.   cm.
Summary: While living in a foster home for girls in
Germany just after World War II, twelve-year-old Halinka carefully
hides her thoughts, feelings, and even her hopes.
[1. Foster home care—Fiction. 2. Child abuse—Fiction.
3. Emotional problems—Fiction. 4. Germany—History—1945–1955—Fiction.]
I. Crawford, Elizabeth D.   II. Title.
PZ7.P921965Wg   1998   [Fic]—dc21   98-16088

ISBN 0-8050-5861-3 / First American Edition—1998
Designed by Martha Rago
Printed in the United States of America on acid-free paper. ∞
10 9 8 7 6 5 4 3 2 1

Contents

HALINKA

those
who can't bite
shouldn't
show
their teeth

*T*here are still two potatoes left. They are almost white and waxy and have blackish spots, but all the same I would like to have one. Or both of them. Carefully I reach out a hand. Then immediately I feel the kick against my shin, and for a moment I see black. Not that it hurts so much, but from rage. I pull myself together, though, and quickly withdraw my hand. "Those who can't bite shouldn't show their teeth," Aunt Lou always says. Duro is just too big for me, so there's no point in biting. She's already fourteen; she's leaving next Easter. She wants to begin an apprenticeship as a seamstress after the home, she says. She takes the dish, lets both potatoes slide out onto her plate, and then tilts the rest of the mustard sauce over them. Inge, at the other end of the table, has taken all this in. She raises her eyebrows and very slightly shrugs her shoulders.

At the next table Fräulein Urban stands up and swings the bell that always sits next to her plate. A dull yellow brass bell with a pattern of engraved flowers and a black handle. Our table falls silent immediately because we can't help hearing the ringing. One table after another grows quiet, until even the last girls in the dining room have shut up.

"Everyone pay attention," says Fräulein Urban. "The girls in the fifth and sixth grades are to come to the handicrafts room at one-thirty. Everyone is to be there!"

Renata, the only one from our room who sits at the table with me and is also going into sixth, presses up close to me. She suddenly looks very small, as if Duro had just kicked her in the shin too. But Renata would never dare grab the last potato.

"You don't have to be afraid," I whisper to her. "The handicrafts room isn't so bad. She just wants to talk to all of us about something. Probably we're going to take a class trip to America, to go rafting on the Mississippi."

Renata doesn't find that funny. She doesn't even laugh. Of course, maybe she hasn't read *Huckleberry Finn*. She pulls her head even deeper between her shoulders, and I'm annoyed at myself for saying anything at all to her.

I'm also annoyed at her. I wasn't going to do anything to her—not me! As far as I'm concerned, she can keep her mouth shut as long as she wants. I don't force myself on anyone. Ever. An important line in my thoughts book reads: "You should never smile at anyone you've never seen at least smile before."

I don't have either table-clearing duty or dishwashing duty today, so I'm in our room early, shortly before one. I sit down on my bed and carefully run my finger over the bump that's growing on my shin. I'm certainly going to have a black-and-blue spot very soon. That big fat cow! I take off my shoes. Naturally, I can't get the right shoe off my foot. This morning the stupid shoelace broke, for the third time, and I had to knot it. Now the knot won't go through the eye and I have to unknot it again. I shove the broken ends into the shoe and then lie down on my bed.

I press my face hard into my beautiful russet-colored bedspread and think about Aunt Lou. I always just think about Aunt Lou. And who else would I think about? There are thoughts that hurt, that make me feel sick. I don't want thoughts like that—those thoughts I push quickly away. But thoughts about Aunt Lou are lovely. As if in the middle of a storm the heavens open up so that you can see a strip of blue sky. Once, when we were in the mountains, Aunt Lou and I, we saw a rainbow.

Aunt Lou got very serious and sang me a song, in Polish. I didn't understand most of it, but it was beautiful. Silently, only in my head, I hum the melody to myself.

At one-thirty Elisabeth says, "Come on, we have to go."

I secretly stroke my bedspread once more. Then I stand up and go to the handicrafts room. I'm holding the pieces of the broken shoelace in my hand.

The handicrafts room is full. Everyone is there, all the girls from the fifth and sixth grades. More than thirty. They're sitting on chairs, tables, even on the window-sills. It's quite noisy. Inge is perched on a table along the wall, beside the door to the luggage storeroom. She waves to me and with her other hand pats the place next to her. There's still room for one more.

Three cardboard cartons are standing on the big, flat cutting table. Fräulein Urban places her hands on them and waits until the room is finally quiet.

"Maybe we got CARE packages from America," Inge whispers. "Imagine, Halinka, CARE packages with chocolate and peanut butter."

"There aren't any CARE packages anymore," I whisper back. "Not for a long time."

Inge shrugs her shoulders. "Well, maybe there's been a miracle. Who knows."

In my thoughts book it says: "You should never hope for a miracle, for then you might count on it really happening." I wrote this one when Aunt Lou went to my guardian for the second time and didn't get me again. She was so sure that time, because she'd actually found a permanent job.

Fräulein Urban raises her hand. "Quiet!" she cries. "Everyone listen for a moment! I have a terrific project for you!"

Inge slides a little closer to me and says softly, "Oh, sure, terrific! If she has a project, it's got to be totally stupid."

Inge can't stand Fräulein Urban. I think she still misses Frau Maurer, the director of the Hildegardis Children's Home, where we both were before. I like Fräulein Urban better, if you can talk about *liking* at all. At least she doesn't keep asking what you're thinking and she doesn't keep trying to hug you and kiss you all the time.

Fräulein Urban claps her hands a few times and everyone quiets down. She tells us about an organization called the Mothers' Convalescent League. It was founded by Frau Elly Heuss-Knapp, the wife of our country's president, in 1950—that's two years ago. I've never heard of this Frau Heuss-Knapp, but the name of Theodor Heuss sounded familiar to me, probably from the radio, but exactly who the country's president is I don't know. Fräulein Urban says this Frau Heuss-Knapp is a good woman and clever and charitable. And we should collect money for the Mothers' Convalescent League, she says, so that poor mothers can convalesce, and Frau Heuss-Knapp will be pleased with us.

"What does that mean, *convalesce*?" Inge asks.

Fräulein Urban explains to her that it means to get healthy. I already knew that, because I was in a home like that once. People also call it a sanatorium, and you get thick butter on bread there and lots of milk to drink every day, and after the noonday dinner you have to lie in a lounge chair all wrapped up outdoors, even when it's cold. I didn't like it in that home because I didn't know anyone, except Hannelore, but she died pretty soon. However, I did convalesce. No wonder, with so much butter! And besides, Aunt Lou visited me once a month. I was there for almost half a year. And two years ago, when Frau Heuss-Knapp—why does she have two last names, anyhow?—founded this thing, I had just come to the home. Not this one, but the Hildegardis Children's

Home, for the little ones. I just came to this one last year, after the Easter holidays. How long I will have to stay, nobody knows. If I'm lucky, Aunt Lou will find a man to marry. Otherwise it could take years. I'd rather not think about that. I can't imagine it, and I don't want to imagine it either.

I look out the window, over the heads of Susanne, Claudia, and the new one in the fifth grade, whose faces I can scarcely make out against the brightness outside—just dark, blurry spots. The sky behind them is blue with a few white clouds, and only the tip of the big chestnut tree in the schoolyard is visible.

"The mothers have to go to the convalescent homes alone, without their children," Fräulein Urban says, "without children, so that they are free of responsibility for a while. Because mothers with several children are overburdened and have to work much too much."

"But she didn't found this whatchamacallit home for *our* mothers," says the new girl in the fifth grade. "Not for *our* mothers."

"Shut up," Susanne says loudly. She doesn't have a mother anymore.

"Your mothers are somewhat different," Fräulein Urban answers. "But imagine a mother with five children, for instance, who has to run from morning till evening and toil and moil and cook for her children and wash, who then needs a chance to rest so that she doesn't collapse."

I can't imagine any mother who cooks and washes all day long, not to mention toiling and moiling from morning till evening, whatever that might mean. I don't know any mothers like that. I don't know many mothers at all except mine, and to tell the truth, I would really rather not know her at all. "Be quiet," Aunt Lou scolds whenever I say anything like that. "Your mother went through very, very difficult times and simply couldn't handle it." But what the difficult times were she never says. "Then why did she act so mean if she knew exactly what it felt like?" I asked once. Aunt Lou pulled me onto her lap and caressed me, and she also cried a little. Then she said, "Your mother has a sick soul. Blows don't only strike the outside, Halinkaleh. They go deeper. They also hit the soul. When someone experiences something bad and cruel, she doesn't automatically turn into a better person because of it. It's just as likely that she will become bad and cruel herself." But she wouldn't say any more than that.

I've thought about that for a long time. I'm not sure that Aunt Lou is right. She could be. After all, she's grown up and I'm not. But I can have my own ideas now.

And when I consider it very carefully, I think it should be the other way around: if someone has experienced something bad herself, so that the blows have even hit her soul, then—especially then—she shouldn't hit others.

"Anyone who has five children has only herself to blame," Inge says venomously. "I don't want any children at all."

I don't know if I want children, and if I do, then only two. My mother had only me, and she never toiled and moiled all day long. I don't know what she's doing now. It has nothing to do with me, in any case. Not anymore. She almost never cooked for me when I was still with her anyway. That's what the lady from the Welfare Office said too. "She doesn't care about the child. She must lose custody. She has neglected the child."

There are words that give me a stomachache and almost make me cry. Just like that. It doesn't matter what's really being said. The word *neglected* is one of them. I bring my hand up to my mouth without being seen and bite hard into my thumb. That always helps when I want to think of something else.

Fräulein Urban is still talking. "Indeed, it is a good work," she says, "and it's rewarding to undertake such things. Therefore, as many of you as possible should volunteer to collect. So, now, who wants to participate?"

Aunt Lou has no children. Perhaps she will have some, now that she has Uncle Sam Silver. No, I hope not. I don't want her to have her own children. Then she might not have time to think about me anymore, if she has to toil and moil the whole day long.

It gets very noisy, with everyone talking at once. "My mother doesn't need any Mothers' Convalescent League," Inge says to me. "She lies in bed until noon every day. At least she always used to. What about yours?"

I can't remember anymore how long my mother stayed in bed in the morning. I only know that in the evenings I had to wait a long time until she finally went to sleep. Then nothing could happen to me anymore. But that's none of Inge's business. That's nobody's business.

I don't understand Inge. She always says just what occurs to her. Just like that, without even thinking. And once when Duro said, "Your mother is an Ami whore," she answered, "Sure, but what can I do about it? Do you think I'm happy about it?" Inge is really one of the most peculiar girls in the home. I never know whether I should think she's good or dumb.

I don't give her any answer at all.

I'd much rather think about Aunt Lou than my mother. If Aunt Lou ever had five children and had to work a lot, I would certainly want her to have a chance to rest. Of course I would want that. So I volunteer. The first. "I'll collect."

"Of course," whispers Elisabeth, loud enough so everyone can hear it. "Gypsies have begging in their blood, everyone knows that."

A few girls giggle. Fräulein Urban gets a crease between her eyebrows, but she acts as if she hasn't heard anything.

I don't let myself show at all that I've heard. That's the best way. Should I perhaps say that we aren't Gypsies at all but Jews? Better not. I think Jews might be even worse than Gypsies. I lower my head and reknot the broken shoelaces firmly. That isn't so easy. I have to knot both ends together one eye lower so that I'll be able to get the shoe off again later. But then there's not enough lace left to tie a bow, only just enough for a knot.

"At the end, whoever has the most money in her box gets a prize," Fräulein Urban says.

"What kind of a prize?" asks Inge.

"A surprise. The local representative of the Mothers' Convalescent League has offered a prize."

That works. Now other volunteers also raise their hands.

But Inge doesn't want to collect, not even for a prize. "I'm not letting myself be sent out to beg," she says with an angry face. "That's why I finally came into the home, so my mother couldn't send me out begging anymore."

"This isn't begging," says Fräulein Urban. "This is collecting donations. For a good cause. And besides, you don't have to participate. This is a voluntary thing. But if you don't collect, of course you can't win a prize."

She talks a long time about Frau Heuss-Knapp and the Mothers' Convalescent League and what a good and praiseworthy thing it is, and then finally she says, "All those who have volunteered to collect, please stay here. The others can go to their rooms. But don't make too much noise. After all, it's still midday rest period."

Fifteen girls stay behind. Only Elisabeth and me from our room. Of course. Renata is nearly dumb and only says the most necessary things; Dorothea almost never goes out, because she doesn't want to be stared at by strangers; Rosemarie is too lazy for anything; Jutta hates any sort of undertaking with more than two people; and Susanne would never in her life do a favor for "others," even if she got something for it. To her, all grown-ups and non–home-children are "others." She hates them, she says. However, she only rarely does us any favors either. Why that's so, I don't know. She probably has her reasons for it. But she's not really mean. If you leave her alone, she'll leave you alone. Susanne was with me in Hildegardis, but we weren't in the same room there. She still has a little sister there she's allowed to visit every four weeks.

Now Fräulein Urban opens up the cardboard cartons. There are collecting boxes inside. Each of us gets one. One of the cartons is left unopened because fewer girls have volunteered than Fräulein Urban expected.

The boxes are metal and have a handle and a slit in the cover for coins. The curved top has been soldered shut so that no one can open it. Of course. Who would give girls from the home an open collecting box? I would have even secured the thing with a padlock. The boxes are bright red and MOTHERS' CONVALESCENT LEAGUE is printed on them in black letters.

"There will be collecting today and tomorrow," Fräulein Urban says. "You will return the boxes on Saturday morning. For these two days you have permission to be out from two-thirty to five. Herr Breitkopf knows about it. You can collect anywhere, in apartment houses or on the street, wherever you want. I wish good luck to all of you. And I trust that you will behave well! I don't want to hear any complaints!"

five minutes
in the
garden of eden
are better than
an entire lifetime
in hell

I take off alone, the others go in twos or threes. I would have gone alone anyway, but no one even asked me.

Herr Breitkopf, the janitor, opens the gate for us. He is small, at least for a man, and his head is so tiny that his eyes have to be very close together for sheer lack of space. But his shoulders are very broad. He is not only the janitor of the home and the school but also the manager of the local gymnastics club. Tuesday evenings they always practice in our gym, and a few girls from the home go regularly. I was there once because Herr Sauer, our gym teacher, said I would have a lot of fun. But I didn't. First of all, I don't like gymnastics on apparatus very much, and second of all, Herr Breitkopf was much too bossy, blowing his whistle all the time and stuff.

Herr Breitkopf and his wife have an apartment in the basement. Frau Breitkopf is responsible for the dishwashing, so none of us can stand her. Dishwashing duty is the worst job in the home.

The sun is shining, and as I pass the second house a dog is barking. I never see him, just hear him. Sometimes he barks late in the evening when we're already in bed. I don't see him this time either; he's behind a closed front door. I imagine the dog as big and black and a little bit scary because he has a loud, deep voice.

I would love to have a dog. Not a yapper like the dog that belongs to Aunt Lou's landlady, that barks at anyone who comes into the house, but a big, wild, black, scary dog whose eyes would glow and whose coat would bristle if anyone tried to hit me. I would only have to say, "Sic 'em!" and he would bite. There really could be a dog like that—more than there could be a cudgel-out-of-the-sack. I do like that Grimm's fairy tale very much, though. Of course I can't imagine a gold-donkey at all, but everything else is very good. Sometimes I wish for a table-set-yourself, and sometimes for the cudgel-out-of-the-sack. I know lots of people I'd let my cudgel go at. At Duro, of course, but especially at Elisabeth. The cudgel might just have to beat her until she was dead. But you aren't supposed to think thoughts like that, or your soul can turn black. Aunt Lou says a person has to take care of his heart and his soul because they are more important than everything else. It's easy enough for her to talk.

An old man comes toward me. I hold my box out to him.

"What's that for?" he asks.

"For the Mothers' Convalescent League," I say and explain the business about the poor mothers who absolutely have to rest once in a while, and how Frau Elly Heuss-Knapp, the wife of the president of our country, intends to help them. But only if enough good-hearted people will contribute something. The mothers will then go to a special home without having to take care of their many children. I speak slowly and clearly and don't stutter at all, although I am saying it all for the first time.

"I've always worked too," the man says gruffly. "And I only had a chance to rest up one single time, in the hospital, when I had my hernia operation. So don't bother me with something like this."

I don't bother him. But after a few steps I turn and yell back at him, "Just think about your own mother sometime! How she always washed and cooked for you! And you must have been a very nasty child!"

He raises his fist threateningly. I clutch the box more tightly to me and run all the way to the railroad station.

I'm breathless when I get there. There aren't as many people at the station plaza as I'd expected, but at the moment it doesn't matter to me. I go inside the station and stand in front of the board where the train departure times are posted. Even though I know by heart when the Saturday trains to Aunt Lou's are. At 2:27 and 7:48. There is also another at 5:15, but it only goes on weekdays and not on Saturdays.

When I come out of the station, the sky has suddenly turned cloudy. Over there Claudia and the new girl in the fifth grade are just coming around the corner. Both are swinging their red collecting boxes. Beside them walks Susanne, without a box. How has she managed to get out of the home without having volunteered to collect? And why is she going with them anyhow? She must have just taken advantage of the chance for an extra outing. If she gets caught, she'll get reception duty again. Oh well, it's none of my business.

But I don't want to run into them. So I quickly dash up Wilhelmstrasse to the big intersection. There are a few stores there. On one side of the street there is a bakery and a butcher shop, and across from them, in a half-bombed-out house, there is a clothing store. In front of the butcher's it smells temptingly of sausage. I stand beside the entrance and hold my box under people's noses. "For the Mothers' Convalescent League," I say. "For the many mothers who urgently need a rest and simply have no money. They can't afford any vacation. Just think of your own mother."

One woman says, "I only need to think about myself; I can't afford vacations either." Nevertheless, she pulls out her coin purse and puts a ten-pfennig coin in my box. The coin rattles loudly. My first money! "Thank you," I say as nicely as I know how. She certainly can't expect anything from the Mothers' Convalescent League anymore; she's too old for children.

I feel sick from the smell of the sausage. Sick from hunger. Why does Duro always have to get the last potato? She is already much fatter than I am. I lean back against the wall of the building and try to imagine that it doesn't smell of sausage here but of roasted semolina soup—I can't stand that stuff at all. If I just *smell* roasted semolina soup I lose my appetite immediately. Strange, but just now I absolutely cannot think of how roasted semolina soup smells. Luckily Inge really loves roasted semolina soup and always exchanges my plate of soup for a half portion of margarine at breakfast the next day.

I should really go away and look for another place, but I can't do it. The sausage smell holds me as tightly as if it had hands. In books, sometimes, it tells how someone is enthralled by something. I—I am enthralled by the smell of sausage. From inside the butcher shop I can hear the voice of the woman behind the counter, "What'll it be, then?" She has an unpleasant voice, quite shrill and penetrating. However, I can only hear her voice—I can't make out the answers of the customers. There's just a murmur. "What'll it be, then?"

A smoked pork chop, I want to say, and make it nice and thick. I have only eaten smoked pork chop once in my life. And that time I couldn't really enjoy it properly, because it was on the trip from the sanatorium to the Hildegardis Children's Home with the lady from Welfare. I was so afraid about the home that I almost couldn't swallow anything. But I have remembered the name. Do ordinary children get smoked pork chops very often? I have no idea; I don't know how they live. "The child has no experience of any normal family life," the lady from Welfare told the judge.

Coins drop into my box. Gradually the rattle begins to sound duller. The bottom of the box must be covered now. Many people have given me something. Meanwhile I get the knack of it. I pull in my cheeks, open my eyes very wide, and raise my shoulders a little. You have to look really miserable and pitiful so that people will feel sorry for you. Then they are more likely to give you something. Mothers with nicely dressed children quickly throw one or two coins into my box, then pull their children away from me, as if I might infect them. In the old days I begged sometimes, when I was hungry, but then the people often chased me away. Now nobody can chase me away, now I have this box in my hand. I'm doing a good work. Just look here, all of you. I'm being an example for the rest of you!

The place beside the butcher shop is good because a lot of people buy meat and sausage. Over and over I hear the woman behind the counter ask, "What'll it be, then? Will there be anything else?"

In the home we only get meat on Sundays, usually soup meat, and very seldom ever a roast with gravy. Two or three times a week there's some kind of a casserole, cabbage, lentils, or beans with a few bits of bacon, if you are lucky; Wednesday evenings it's three slices of cold cuts for each person; sometimes for noonday dinner there are hard-boiled eggs with mustard sauce, often on Thursdays or Fridays; and aside from that, it's always just potatoes with vegetables, rice pudding, semolina pudding, noodles. Many in the home say that Frau Koch, our cook, eats the meat that's supposed to go to us. That could be so; she is very fat, and most of us are pretty thin. But I don't believe it all the same. Frau Koch is really very nice, and when you have to do kitchen duty because you've gotten into trouble, she always gives you something to eat.

"Please contribute to the Mothers' Convalescent League," I call and hold up the box.

Again a lady puts a coin in the slot before she goes into the butcher shop. Nevertheless, tomorrow I will look for another spot, because the smell is just driving me crazy.

When the shadow of the building on the other side of the street grows so long that it is creeping up to me across the edge of the sidewalk, I ask a man who has just put a coin in my box what time it is. "Just after four-thirty," he says.

I go into the butcher shop. The floor is tiled, alternating red speckled and yellow speckled. The woman with the loud, shrill voice is fat and gray-haired and has a little mole on the left side of her nose. Her white apron over her blue-striped dress has reddish spots on both sides where she wipes her hands. Blood spots from cutting meat. "What'll it be, then?" she asks. Exactly the same way as I've heard her say it at least a hundred times. But this time she means me.

I hold the box out toward her and say my little speech. But I can't take my eyes off the glass case while I'm doing

it. Fleischwurst, salami, liverwurst, blood sausage, cerve-
lat, headcheese, and other sausages whose names I don't
even know. Sausage, sausage, sausage. And even ham.

The woman leans over the counter and puts something in my box. "Would you like a piece of sausage?"
she asks.

I can only nod; I can't get a single word out.

"Which one do you like the best?" she asks.

I am alarmed. What's that supposed to mean? Why
doesn't she just give me a piece? Is she trying to make
fun of me? Didn't she really mean it, about the sausage? I
feel the tears coming to my eyes.

"Don't worry, child," she says, and all at once her
voice is much deeper and very gentle. She holds out a big
piece of fleischwurst toward me. At least four inches
long. "Here," she says. "And where are you from? From
the home?" Her voice keeps getting gentler.

I nod and clutch the sausage. Suddenly I have so much
saliva in my mouth that I can't even say "thank you."
The woman is looking at me very kindly. "Come by
again tomorrow," she says in that other voice, her second one. And then I can finally say "thank you," and
"good-bye."

On the way home I very slowly suck the fleischwurst

out of the skin. So slowly that I have to make a detour around by the freight train station, which begins not far beyond our playing fields. "Five minutes in the Garden of Eden are better than an entire lifetime in Hell," Aunt Lou says when she eats something especially good. And then, just before our gate, I also put the skin in my mouth, chew it thoroughly, and swallow it down before I ring the bell.

I put the box on my night table beside my favorite book, *The Adventures of Huckleberry Finn*. I keep taking it out each time; sometimes I don't read it at all, but I like having it lying next to my bed. Perhaps sometime I'll tell the woman at the library that I've lost it. Perhaps a miracle will happen and she'll say, "That's not so bad, child, we'll just buy a new one." And if I have to pay for the book, then I can always say I've suddenly found it again. I'll see.

I sit down at the desk and begin my homework.

Elisabeth goes past me to my night table and, without asking, lifts my box, checking its weight. She looks envious as she moves her hand back and forth, testing. "Yours is heavier," she says. "No wonder."

This time she doesn't say anything about Gypsies. Although it wouldn't have bothered me so much now.

Anyhow, I have a big piece of fleischwurst in my stomach. Of course I don't say a word about that. I'm not stupid, after all!

Tomorrow I might just try the bakery. Who knows—I might get a roll to go with the sausage. It could happen.

one who is poor needn't fear thieves

The bedtime gong rang a long time ago. I take off my bedspread. It really belongs to me. Hardly anything else does. All I have left from before is my old schoolbag, which is already so worn that in many places the bare cardboard is showing, and the pocketknife that Arnulf gave me. "Don't worry about it," Aunt Lou would say. "One who is poor needn't fear thieves."

But that's not right, I think. A poor person is just the one to be afraid that the little he has can be stolen. A rich person might not care if someone swipes something from him. You can bet he has more than enough of it anyhow. A rich person only needs to snap his fingers and immediately he has what he wants. I would die of grief if someone were ever to take away my bedspread. Maybe a rich person also has only one, but he can buy a new one anytime. I couldn't. I don't have any money.

And it wasn't easy for Aunt Lou to pay for my bedspread that time when I had just gone into the home, into the Hildegardis. The very first time I was allowed to visit her, she said, "I'll buy you a beautiful bedcover so that your bed will look pretty and you won't forget me." Of course she hadn't really meant the second reason seriously. I could never forget Aunt Lou, or want to forget her, which she knew very well.

We went to Herrling's store and the saleslady said that these covers were called bedspreads. Mine is russet-brown with tiny little flowers. "A practical pattern," Aunt Lou said. "It won't show the dirt so much." There was also a yellow one, a cowslip-yellow one, that I really would much rather have had. But there was nothing to be done about it, and finally Aunt Lou paid for the spread. Might makes right—I knew that even then, although I was still pretty dumb.

Therefore my bedspread is russet-brown with little ochre flowers and tiny green leaves that are so small you can hardly see the green. The pattern really is practical. But also I'm careful and never lie on the bed with my shoes on. Really never. I'd even prefer to take my dress off so that no dirt at all gets on my bedspread, but it usually isn't warm enough for that. And besides, my gym shorts are often dirtier than my dress. I carefully fold up the bedspread and hang it over the back of my chair.

Dorothea, who sleeps in the bed next to mine, is rummaging around in her treasure box. It's a wooden box in which she keeps her secret things. Nobody knows exactly what all is in there, except maybe Elisabeth, her friend. Every now and then Dorothea shows us something, such as an amber bead or a postage stamp or a ring, but then she puts it right back again. And there's no chance for a secret look. The treasure box has a lock, and Dorothea wears the key on a cord around her neck.

"Do you think you'll win the prize?" she asks. "I would love to know what it is."

I shrug. I hope that I'll win it; I'm even trying very hard to. But I would never say it out loud. I can just imagine how they would make fun of me if I failed. No, I'm not going to say anything. But I intend to get the prize, even if I don't know what it is. Maybe chocolate? A book? Or watercolors? Perhaps even a wonder ball. Jutta got one of those from her grandma for her birthday. It's a ball of wool with knitting needles and when you've knitted all the wool you find a present inside. But Jutta didn't knit; she just unwound the ball. There was a five-mark coin inside. She was really happy and on Sun-

day she went to the movies and saw *Double Lottie.*
Afterwards she told us the entire story. The girls who
play the main roles are twins. "And one of them is
named Jutta," Jutta said proudly.

Dorothea snaps her treasure box shut and locks it.
Then she lifts up my box and shakes it. It rattles loudly.

"Quiet!" Elisabeth yells. She's lying on her bed by the
window, a book in her hand and her stupid doll in her
arms. No one else is ever allowed to touch this doll, and
she watches very carefully. I don't think I ever had a doll;
at least I don't remember ever having one. Beside her,
in the middle of her night table, stands her red Mothers'
Convalescent League collecting box.

Suddenly I have an idea. I don't want to be distrustful,
but you never know. I take my pocketknife out of my
schoolbag, take my collecting box out of Dorothea's
hands, and carefully scratch an *H* into the red paint.
Small and way down, but visible. "So that it doesn't get
mixed up by mistake," I say very loudly, loudly enough
so that Elisabeth certainly hears. "After all, the collecting boxes all look the same."

"Sometimes you are really very clever," Susanne says
from her bed by the door, and I hand the box back to
Dorothea.

Could be that Aunt Lou is right about the rich who are afraid of being robbed. But of course the box doesn't belong to me; it belongs to the Mothers' Convalescent League. Or to the local representative, who has offered the prize. I decide the prize must be chocolate.

Dorothea puts the box back on my night table and carries her treasure box to the wardrobe. Before she climbs back into bed, she shakes my box once more.

"Quiet!" bellows Elisabeth, so loudly now that Jutta starts in her sleep. "Just be quiet, I want to finish my chapter!"

Jutta is already asleep, as usual. She's always the first one to go to bed, and she falls asleep so fast that we've stopped being worried about her. Actually, we never *were* worried about her, and when you come right down to it, in Jutta's case, there's no reason to—she's anything but strong. She's even smaller than I am, only not so thin, so she's no threat to anyone.

I undress and put on my nightie.

The door opens. "Not all of you are in bed yet," Fräulein Urban says, "and the gong rang ten minutes ago. Now hurry up, if you don't want a demerit."

I make a leap and pull the covers up to my chin.

"Did you wash, or did you just get into bed as

you are?" asks Fräulein Urban. "After all, I know my girls."

"I was in the bathroom before," I murmur. And I don't even blush when I say it.

"That's all right, then," she says. "Elisabeth, put the book away. Good night, children."

The light goes out. At first it's very dark in the room. Then my eyes get used to it and the black turns to a dusky gray. We don't have any window shutters, only beige curtains, and when the moon shines, it's so bright in the room that I can make out the others in their beds.

"Always at the most exciting place," growls Elisabeth through the darkness. "I really don't understand at all why we can't have lamps on our night tables."

No one says anything. What can you say to such a dumb remark? Why should anyone buy bedside lamps for us? Besides, electricity costs money. I lie in bed and stare at the ceiling, the way I do every night. I can only fall asleep after the others are asleep; I don't even know why that is. It's been that way from the beginning, and it hasn't changed.

I think about the film that Jutta saw. Two girls meet in a vacation home. What is that anyhow? Who would voluntarily go into a home when they are on vacation? Jutta said it was different from ours, and all the girls were very beautifully dressed. Could be. After all, it was a movie. Both girls look exactly the same, and then it turns out that they are twins. One lived with the father and one with the mother, and of course everything turns out well and in the end all four are together again, the twins and their parents. I imagine that I have a twin sister who looks exactly like me. But she doesn't live with any old father but with very rich, nice people. Suddenly I get such a rush of anger at her that I could howl. I see her right there in front of me, in a cowslip-yellow dress with a white ribbon in her hair. She's laughing. She's laughing at me. Fury rises up into my head and presses against the backs of my eyes. I hate her, my sister, because she has it so good.

Jutta coughs in her sleep, and suddenly I have to laugh. I don't even have a sister!

Susanne is falling asleep; she's already tossing back and forth all the time. First head and shoulders, then only her head. Sometimes it lasts forever, but sometimes it's over very quickly. Soon I hear Elisabeth snoring softly. Her snoring gets on my nerves. But she can't do anything about it; she has polyps. There is nothing to be heard from Rosemarie's bed, not even a rustle.

And then Renata begins to cry. That is the worst, because then I have to quickly think of something very beautiful or I will have to cry too. Every night, Renata weeps softly, almost silently, but the longer she cries, the louder it sounds to me. And the harder it is for me to think of something else. I would prefer to think of the sausage, but then I wouldn't be able to fall asleep at all, because I am hungry again. Thinking about food before falling asleep at night is really the dumbest thing a person can do. I know all about that.

So I think about orchids. I have no idea what they look like; I only know them from reading about them. They must be very beautiful, because the word sounds so beautiful. Orchids. Orrr-chids. I imagine that anyone who sees one is spellbound. Certainly they have large, delicate flowers. Not bright and explosive like the flowers that grow in some front gardens, such as tulips. No, they must be very delicate. Violet, crimson, purple. I asked Fräulein Urban what crimson is, and she showed me the color in a book of paintings with lots of pictures. Crimson is a dark red, a very warm red. The crimson in the book was bright, but that could have been the paper. Orchids are certainly not bright. They are delicate and soft and so sensitive that they get dark spots if you touch them. A little like autumn crocus, only much bigger and more magical. At least that's how I imagine them. They grow in the tropics. Where the tropics are exactly I don't know either, but far away.

Elfriede was in Italy last summer. Her mother's latest friend has a car. In Italy there are palm trees, Elfriede said. I've never seen a palm tree. Aunt Lou said someday, when she earns a lot of money, we'll also go to Italy, just the two of us. And then she described to me exactly what it looks like. The sea blue-green to the horizon, the beach of fine, almost white sand, and tall, slender palms under a bright blue sky. And the nights! Millions of stars in a sky of black velvet. She described it all as if she'd grown up in Italy. And she has never been there either. But she knew exactly how it looked, she said, and someday . . .

Renata has stopped crying. She's asleep. There is nothing more to be heard in the room, no rustling, just breathing and Elisabeth's soft snoring. I wish I knew if Rosemarie's asleep. But with her you can never be certain. She has the bed across from mine, so I can't see her either. I hold my breath and try to listen for her breathing. She appears to be asleep. But perhaps she's just pretending to be. I'd better wait a while longer.

Then I begin to count. Sometimes I know the next morning how far I got with the counting the night before, but usually I've forgotten.

he who
dreams of palaces
loses his place
in the hut

I keep counting and counting, but it doesn't do any good. I simply cannot fall asleep. The evenings and nights in the home are especially bad. Particularly if a person has trouble falling asleep. And the more I try, the more wide awake I become. So I'll have to go to my secret place for a little while. I immediately feel better. But still I wait a few more minutes, to be certain that they all really are asleep.

In my secret place I keep my thoughts book, where I write all the important sayings that come to me. I wouldn't be so stupid as to leave the book here in the room, where someone could find it. Elisabeth, for instance. I can just imagine what would happen then. She would read my sayings out loud to everyone and laugh herself sick. "Listen to this: 'The mouse only needs to see the cheese and already she is stumbling into the trap.' Ha ha ha, the Gypsy must think she's a poet! She thinks she's just so smart! Ha ha ha!"

Of course, Elisabeth wouldn't understand a single word of it anyway. Luckily, or she would laugh even louder. I actually wrote that saying the time she intentionally left a fifty-pfennig piece lying on the shelf beneath her desk. She is really mean. Fräulein Urban found the coin in my schoolbag. It didn't do any good to say that I'd found it on the street. Elisabeth had filed a mark in the edge, and Dorothea saw her do it. Why hadn't I noticed that? I ought to have seen the mark. I always notice things like that. I got two weeks of kitchen duty as punishment, and Elisabeth said loudly, "So there you are—all Gypsies steal."

Since then I have been more careful, much more careful. That's why my book of thoughts stays where it is, even if I would sometimes like to have it with me in order to write something, or only to thumb through it for a while.

I could find the way to my secret place in my sleep, I've been there so often. Sometimes I take a book with me, or even paper and pencil to write a letter to Aunt Lou. I often write her letters at night, though I rarely

send them to her. I don't want her to have even more
worries about me. It doesn't do any good, because she
can't change anything. At least until she gets married.
But I'd rather not think about that, since I was already
mistaken once. Last winter Aunt Lou got to know a
man, an engineer, and she said perhaps he might be the
right one. But after going dancing with him three times
it was over. Why, I didn't know; she didn't tell me and I
didn't ask.

Now everyone is certainly asleep, even Rosemarie. I
quietly climb out of bed. Just in case, I take a pencil and
my arithmetic notebook with me. I just began a new
one, so I can easily pull out the two middle pages in case
I change my mind and write to Aunt Lou. In the corridor
I stick close to the wall, for in the middle there are lots
of places where the boards creak. They sound very loud
at night. The big clock reads a few minutes before ten.

Up ahead, in the hallway that is separated from our
corridor by a glass door, there is a bulb that burns all
night so that we don't have to turn on a light if we go
to the bathroom. The few steps across the lighted hallway to the short passageway that leads to the handicrafts room are the most dangerous part of the journey
because Fräulein Urban could suddenly come out of her
apartment.

Fräulein Urban lives right next to us, you see, in the home. She has no family, only a friend who comes to see her very often. This friend always wears gray and lilac and has her hair pulled together in a severe knot at the back of her neck. She's known to everyone in the home only as "the lilac-gray oh-god-oh-god," and everyone laughs at her because she has such a strange way of speaking. As if she's going to sing or is about to recite a poem. Duro often imitates her "oh-god-oh-god" during meals, especially if Inge is wearing her lilac sweater. "Oh-god-oh-god, Inge, but you're looking elegant today."

Then I turn into the corridor off the hallway and softly open the door to the handicrafts room. Made it. Or almost, at least.

The curtains in the handicrafts room are never drawn, and a little light comes through the windows from the streetlamps behind the schoolyard. I can see well enough not to worry that I will bump against a table or trip over a stool by mistake. Now really nothing can happen anymore. I cross the room and stand in front of the door to the luggage storeroom. It's locked, as always, but I know where the key is. Way up on the shelves where the cartons with scissors, knitting needles, and sewing things are is a paper envelope in which the key is kept. If a person stands on a stool, it's easy to get.

The lock and the hinges to the door used to squeak very loudly, so I put some machine oil on them a few months ago. It was in a little can with a long spout above the top. Then at the end of the spout there was another little cover to take off. I borrowed the can one evening from Herr Breitkopf's workshop and put it back again the next noon. He hadn't noticed it at all, I guess, or at least it didn't cause any trouble. Since I oiled the door thoroughly, it doesn't squeak anymore and opens and closes very easily.

I immediately lock the door behind me with the key. I have no desire to get caught. That would be the end of my secret place.

It's dark here in the storeroom, for unfortunately the huge roof has only two tiny little trap windows. They are only for ventilation, but that's unnecessary in any case because there is already enough air coming in through the cracks between the roof tiles. During the day there's a little bit of light, but all the same Fräulein Urban always takes a flashlight with her when she gets one of our suitcases out. I've solved the problem of the darkness. I pat my hands along the wall to the right until I find the beam behind which my treasure lies hidden under old newspapers: many candles, twenty-seven exactly, large and small, thick and thin, some only stubs, and two packages of matches.

I sneaked the candles from various Advent wreaths and Christmas trees last winter, from the classroom, from Fräulein Urban, and from the home's Christmas tree, and the matches from Frau Breitkopf, who always has some in her apron pocket to light the gas stove in the dishwashing room. After work she always takes off her apron and hangs it over a chair while she combs her hair in front of the mirror above the sink. You only have to know what you want, then you can find an opportunity to get it. Sometimes, anyhow. I even have a small flashlight. It was lying in the hallway in school on a windowsill, and I just put it away. But unfortunately the batteries ran out a long time ago, and I have no money for new ones. It's of no use to me anymore.

I light a candle, one of the fat ones. Now I don't have to be quiet; no one can hear me here very easily. Except for the mice, but they won't do anything to me; I hear them rustling sometimes.

Way back under the slant of the roof I have arranged a little place for myself. I piled a few suitcases on top of one another, a little untidily, so that the whole thing looks accidental and not as if it was done especially to hide something. Behind the wall of suitcases there is an old gray wool blanket with two brown stripes along the edge. Aunt Lou has one just like it, only without burn holes, and she calls it a *koldra*. I cover myself up with Aunt Lou's koldra when I sleep with her. I found my koldra in the laundry room in the basement. Maybe no one wanted it because it was really old and had a few little holes in it. They don't bother me. When it's warm I can sit on my koldra, and when it's cold I can wrap myself in it. It's lovely here, especially when there's a candle burning. I sit as if I were in a little cave. All I can see is a wooden joist and the back of the suitcase wall.

The luggage storeroom is really a wonderful hiding place. Since I got the idea to set up my nest there, things have gone a little better for me in the home, at least at night after lights-out. Too bad I can't go there in the daytime, but then certainly someone would find out about it. Besides, by daylight the luggage storeroom would look more like a storeroom.

I put the candle on the koldra and get my thoughts book out of its hiding place under a few old roof tiles. My thoughts book is actually a poetry album. Aunt Lou gave it to me for my birthday last year and said, "Let all your friends write in it, Halinka. Later, when you are a grown woman, you will be happy when you look through it and remember them."

Strange. Where did she get the idea that I could have friends? I've never had a friend. I don't want any, either. If you watch Elisabeth and Dorothea, who are supposed to be friends, you could really lose interest in friendship. Elisabeth always gets Dorothea to do her work—room duty, tidying up the wardrobe, reception duty. Everything except dishwashing duty. Dorothea has a hunchback. Really, people call it a hump. Anyhow, she isn't allowed to wash dishes, for during the washing a person has to stand bent over for a long time, sometimes more than an hour, and even my back hurts afterwards. One time Elisabeth tried to talk me into doing dishwashing duty for her. She offered me candy out of the package she gets from home every two weeks. Since then I know why Dorothea does everything for Elisabeth. Not me; I spat at her feet. Complete scorn; somewhere I read about doing that.

No, I don't need any friends, and I certainly don't want to remember them all later. I want to forget them. I don't like many people, and they like me even less, I imagine. I think Renata is very nice, although she never has anything to say except ordinary things like "What time is it?" or "What's for dinner today?" or "There's a light-bulb out in the bathroom." Since Renata came, I think much more often about orchids. I don't know why. Perhaps because she looks so brownish and gentle. She has light-brown hair, light-brown eyes, and a light-brown skin. Still, I don't quite understand it, for orchids are violet, purple, and crimson.

I reach for my secret smelling bottle, a bottle of Pelikan Oil. The stuff is still quite new; I just managed to get it two weeks ago and then threw away the old bottle, which hardly had any smell left anymore. Slowly I unscrew the cover and hold the bottle up to my nose. I am utterly wild about the smell of Pelikan Oil. What a fragrance! A little like marzipan, and a little like something strange, mysterious. When I smell Pelikan Oil, I can forget the home and everything else. I didn't used to know that there was such a marvelous smell until Fräulein Urban helped us make decorations for Christmas. Sometimes I put just a little bit of Pelikan Oil on the back of my hand with the little brush that is in the bottle before I go back to bed again. Then I can smell it while I'm counting.

No, I don't want Renata to become my friend. Why should I make life unnecessarily difficult for myself? What's the good of a friend who isn't strong? It stands to reason, someone like that can only make trouble for a person.

However, I would take her as a little sister immediately. Perhaps I might be able to teach her how not to cry anymore? I have much more experience than she does; of course I am at least half a year older than she is. Renata is one of the youngest girls in our class.

Crying in bed every night! Whoever did anything like that? Although I sometimes suspect that she cries because she thinks everyone except her is asleep. That could be good; no one notices that I'm still awake. I can lie completely quiet and breathe evenly. I've practiced it long enough. By the way, Rosemarie can do it just as well as I can.

Rosemarie would have been a useful friend. She's quite large and strong. And she doesn't let anything go by. Even Elisabeth doesn't dare to do anything to her. She also looks pretty. But she's dumb, I think. Anyhow, she's very bad in school. But she doesn't care, she's going to inherit the café someday, so she doesn't need good grades, she says. Her mother has a café that stays open all night, which is why Rosemarie is here in the home. She says it's a café and Elisabeth says it's a bordello. A bordello is a house where men come because they want to make love to women. Elisabeth says "to screw." I don't know what that's supposed to mean. Or at least not exactly, only sort of. Aunt Lou said *screw* is a bad word and that I'm not allowed to use it. I should say a man and a woman "make love to each other." Sometimes Aunt Lou is like a child, and there are things she simply doesn't understand. No one can put anything over on me so easily. Later, when I'm grown up, I'm going to watch out for Aunt Lou so that nobody hurts her.

Rosemarie has reddish hair and very white skin, and she doesn't tan in summer. I think she is the prettiest girl in the entire home. She knows how pretty she is. At home, in her mother's café, all the men run after her, she says. She has breasts already. I don't yet, although lately my nipples are getting a little fatter. But they are light pink and no bigger than my little fingernail, and hers are very large and dark brown.

Rosemarie is a problem for me. A much bigger problem than Elisabeth. Elisabeth is simply mean, and you don't expect purring from a wolf. Rosemarie isn't mean, not really mean. She's indifferent.

Sometimes at night she'll wait until the others are asleep, then suddenly she's standing beside my bed. I feel her even before I see her. Without saying anything, she will sit on my bed, shove the covers aside, and lie down beside me. I know exactly what she wants, even though I can't remember that she ever said anything to me. I don't even know anymore when the first time was. But I know exactly what she wants.

She lies on her stomach, her nightie pulled up to her neck, and I stroke her back. Not with my whole hand, just with my fingertips. Very softly and gently. She likes it that way. She never says a word, but I know from the way she moves under my fingertips that I am doing it right. That it pleases her. Her skin feels soft and warm and wonderful. She isn't fat, actually she's really thin, but nothing about her is bony, not even her knees. And even her shoulder blades are soft. When I get close to the place below her armpits, she will move her arm to the side. I know that; it's the same every time. I move my fingertips to the place between her shoulder blades and armpit, there, where she already has tiny, curly hairs. And then a little deeper. Just to the place where her breast begins to get round. She says nothing. She lies very still. I never know what she's thinking. Maybe she isn't thinking anything at all. Rosemarie the Dumb. Sometimes I get so angry that I would rather hit her, but of course I don't do that. Maybe she isn't dumb at all. Maybe that's just her trick for keeping the others in check.

But if she wants something from me, why doesn't she say so? She never says anything. Never, never, never. Sometimes she hugs me and presses herself very hard against me. We will lie like that for a very long time. But the next morning it's always as if nothing has happened. As if she hadn't been lying next to me. And when Elisabeth makes a stupid remark about Gypsies, Rosemarie will laugh along with her.

Sometimes I like her very much because she is so beautiful; anyhow, I always like to look at her. And maybe she could have been my friend if she didn't forget everything the next morning.

Incidentally, she never caresses me. That's perfectly all right with me. I'm afraid she would ask where my scars came from. But luckily she doesn't do it. She goes back to her bed again, and I stay behind, alone. On those nights when she comes to me under the covers, I feel really alone afterwards. Then I do wish for a friend. But not for very long. In the morning, after we get up, I don't look over to her bed, but when I hear her voice I begin to tremble. That lasts for at least half a day. She never says anything special to me. She doesn't talk very much anyway. But how did she know that I am someone you could do something like that with? "Gypsies are all whores,"

Elisabeth says. "Any man can buy them if he just pays enough."

Rosemarie never looks at me during the day. During the day she looks right through me. Sometimes, when she hasn't come to me for a whole week or two, I ask myself who she's been going to instead. Although I know perfectly well that I'm always the last to fall asleep, I then look at the other girls in the room and think, Not to them. I'm very sure of that. She isn't going to any of them. But she also hasn't come to me for a very long time.

Yesterday I saw her with Duro. They were sitting together near the ball fields and talking very eagerly together. Duro, of all people, that fat cow! I don't care.

I lay the Pelikan Oil bottle aside, open my thoughts book, and write something important in it: "A person should never wish for something impossible. He who dreams of palaces loses his place in the hut." Then I reach for my bottle again. I'll just smell it a bit more before I go to bed.

he who intends
to kill a fat goose
must first
feed it well

ext morning in school I can't pay attention at all. I keep thinking about collecting. About collecting and the prize. Somehow I have to get people to put more money in my box than in any of the others. "He who intends to kill a fat goose must first feed it well," Aunt Lou says. And I do intend to kill a fat goose. I want the prize! I must have it! Maybe the prize will be a book? Maybe a big box of watercolors like the one Rosemarie has? It has twenty-four different colors in it.

Then I have a magnificent idea.

During recess I sneak into the handicrafts room without anyone seeing me and slip a piece of drawing charcoal out of the drawer. I will use it to make dark rings under my eyes, and then I will look even more pitiful. Then the mothers with their prettily dressed children will have to put even more money in my box. Wow! Serves them right. Why I don't know, but it really does serve them right! I can't stand mothers with prettily dressed children.

During fifth period we got back the dictation that we'd written the week before. Too bad, I got a D. But I could have expected it. I'm bad in dictation. Maybe it's because I first went to school in Poland and only learned German later. Or maybe I'm just too stupid for dictation. Otherwise I'm very good in school, especially in composition and arithmetic. But I make an effort, too, because Aunt Lou wants me to.

At noon, the mail is handed out to us before we eat. Fräulein Urban has the letters lying on the table in front of her and calls each person up. This time there is actually a letter for me there, the letter I've been waiting for for so long. From Aunt Lou, of course. Who else? A longish brown envelope. I put on an indifferent face when I take it, but my hand is trembling.

The others tear their letters open immediately and begin to read as they walk. I would never do that. My letters belong to me, just to me alone. People shouldn't see how glad I am, not even for one minute. I hold the envelope up to the light just very briefly. But the paper is too thick, and I can't see what's in it.

"Well, Halinka, don't you want to open your letter and read it?" Fräulein Urban asks.

I don't answer her. I stick the envelope under my red blouse, which Aunt Lou bought for me at Easter vacation, and quickly sit down in my place. I act as if it were nothing special, but I am singing inside. Aunt Lou, Aunt Lou, Aunt Lou! I have been waiting so long for this letter.

Inge has gotten a little package. "From my mother," she says and lays it beside her plate.

Duro asks her why she doesn't open it right away, but Inge isn't so dumb. So that she has to give Duro something from it? She only shakes her head.

Who knows what-all there will be in the package. Candies, of course; there are candies in all packages. Sometimes also chocolate or a book or something to wear. Elisabeth recently got a brown bouclé top and a green scarf to go with it.

The letter from Aunt Lou rustles under my blouse, but so softly that I am the only one who hears it. Letters from Aunt Lou are beautiful. Not because she writes long letters about something that's happened, a story or something like that. She never does that because actually she can't write German very well, and I have almost forgotten my Polish. The main thing is, Aunt Lou is the only one who writes to me; otherwise I have nobody. And besides, there is always something in her letters. At least almost always. Sometimes a five-mark note and sometimes a tenner, which is then for a train ticket. This time there will be a ten-mark note inside, I am sure of that. And then on the weekend I will go to stay with her. Just in time; I can hardly stand it here anymore.

Every four weeks you can go home for the weekend, and it's been so long since I've been to Aunt Lou's. It wasn't possible during Whitsun vacation because the woman who is her landlady had her son and daughter-in-law and their children visiting. The house was too full and so she wouldn't give permission for me to come.

Aunt Lou visited me on Whitsunday, and we went for a long walk. Straight through the forest to the pub at the lookout. We had lemonade there, and then we walked back again. Toward evening Aunt Lou went away again, and I was left all alone here. I have now been in the home for almost nine weeks without break; this weekend will be the ninth.

After dinner I go right to the toilet, carefully lock the door, and tear open the envelope. No ten-mark note, not even a fiver. No money at all, only a very short letter.

She has not been able to work for two weeks because she had the flu, so she can't send me any money yet. Now she is well again. "You must just have a little patience," she writes. But she loves me very much and sends me many kisses, and Uncle Sam Silver also sends me greetings.

A beautiful letter, even if it's so short. I can't help crying a little. Whether from joy or disappointment I don't know myself. I would so love to go to Aunt Lou.

Outside, someone is banging on the door. I don't bother about her for a while; I hate it when I have to hurry like that. And I hate it most of all when someone can see that I've been crying. Slowly I fold up the letter, put it back in its envelope, and then put the envelope inside my undershirt. That's a secure place. The belt to my skirt is tight enough to keep the envelope from slipping out. It feels cool and a little scratchy.

Someone is banging on the door again, or, more precisely, hammering. Such a stupid cow, out there. She could still have gone to the other end of the corridor; there are two toilets right next to each other there.

"I love you very much," Aunt Lou wrote. At the very

beginning, when I had just come into the home, she wrote *luv* instead of *love*. *Love* is spelled with an *o* and an *e*, I answered, and she wrote back that she would remember that. *Love* is a very important word, and one should not write it wrong.

There is pounding again, and someone screams, "Hurry up and come out of there!"

Of course I recognize the voice immediately. It's Elfriede. If only I had known that! I would never have started anything with her, she's much too big and strong, and she starts hitting for any little thing. Why didn't she say who she was? I still sometimes forget that there are a great many here who are bigger and stronger than I am. In Hildegardis it was different; there I was one of the big ones.

Now I really do hurry. When I open the door, I pull in my head and hold my hands in front of my face. So Elfriede only gets me once on the left cheek, but it's a good one.

"Next time you come right out when someone else has to go, understand?" Then she runs right into the toilet and doesn't even shoot the bolt, she's in such a hurry. Luckily she's so mad she doesn't look at me very carefully. She certainly doesn't notice that my eyes are red from crying.

I go into the washroom and look at myself in the mirror. My eyes are red, but at the moment no one would notice that, for my cheek is even redder and is swelling. The fingermarks are already showing as white streaks. In an hour, at most, they will be gone again, I know that. On me, every blow and every scratch show twice as clearly as on the others.

"That's an allergic reaction," the doctor in the sanatorium said. "Your skin is extremely sensitive to any irritation."

Aunt Lou, who was there, stroked my hand and said, "Her soul too."

The doctor looked at her as if she were cracked. It's always a little painful to me when Aunt Lou says something like that in front of strangers. But when we are alone I love to listen to her. She says such beautiful things.

Sometimes an allergic reaction like that is useful too. Last year a substitute teacher who didn't know me boxed my ears, I don't remember why. Anyhow, my cheek swelled up and got so red, and you could see all the fingermarks very clearly. He stared at me in complete horror, then he brought me up into the home's infirmary and said I should lie down and rest. Naturally I rested the entire morning; I would have been really stupid if I hadn't. At noon the girl on infirmary duty brought me something to eat, and I just lay there in bed until evening and read. Then Fräulein Urban showed up before supper and chased me down to the dining room. She knows about my allergic reactions and doesn't take them particularly seriously. And I can understand that too.

I wash my eyes with cold water until it almost doesn't show that I've been crying, then I go to our room. Only Elisabeth, Susanne, and Renata are there. Elisabeth is lying on her bed, and she keeps changing her doll's clothes. Renata looks at me in horror, and Susanne asks who did it. "Elfriede," I say and lie down on my bed. My cheek burns, my eyes burn, and my stomach hurts. Maybe I'm getting sick.

I'm often sick. I have some kind of illness for which Dr. Zuleger, our doctor, doesn't have a name. That's what he says, anyway. When I'm sick, I have to vomit, my stomach hurts, my head—just everything. And I am so tired that I sleep all the time. I sleep and cry. Then after two or three days I've slept and cried enough and everything is normal again. Earlier, in Hildegardis, it was much worse than here. "You're getting older," Dr. Zuleger said, "and someday it will be gone entirely." I hope he's right!

I press my face into my bedspread. The next time I'm

with Aunt Lou, I'm going to ask her to give me a little of her perfume again, and then I'll put it on my bedspread so that it smells of her. "You have a nose like a fox and eyes like an eagle," Aunt Lou said to me one time. "You will always get along somehow." I felt a little proud when she said that.

But it's so, I really do have a good nose. And by the way, here's something strange that I've noticed. It's easy to recall things you see or hear. Smells are trickier. But when you smell a certain thing again, you suddenly remember that you know it and don't understand at all how you ever could have forgotten it.

When I hear Elisabeth take her box and head for the door, I know that it must be just before two-thirty, because Elisabeth has her very own wristwatch. I wait until the door closes behind her, then I get up. I go to the washroom again, to the mirror, with my piece of charcoal. The slap mark on my cheek is gone. I draw fantastic dark rings under my eyes. Then I wipe a little of the color off with the bottom of my skirt because the rings look a little too black to me. Now I have black stripes on my right cheek. I wipe and draw and draw and wipe until finally I'm satisfied. If I hold my face very close to the mirror, I can of course see the charcoal lines, but when I move back two or three steps, it looks very real. A pitiful girl with deep rings under her eyes. I just have to be careful to keep my head down if anyone is standing very close to me. But from a distance it is terrifically effective.

Then I grab my box and run out. The door to the reception room is open. As I go by I see that Herr Sauer is supervising today. He never bothers about anything. "The main thing is to keep the noise within limits," he always says. "Everything else is all right with me." And that's how he acts too. If any of us ever has any plans—to go out without permission, or something like that—then she waits until Herr Sauer is on duty.

All the teachers have to take turns doing afternoon supervision in the home. The worst is Frau Knieser. When she's on, she keeps sneaking around the corridors, just lurking until she finds us doing something forbidden. But Frau Knieser is rarely on duty because she has a sick mother at home she has to take care of. Or, maybe she only says that because she doesn't like to supervise us. You can never rely on us, she says. She would rather herd a sack full of fleas.

I wouldn't want to work in the home either. Anything but that. I wouldn't go into any home of my own free will.

when good fortune comes calling, open the door

Herr Breitkopf opens the door for me. "You're late," he says. "The others are all long gone."

What's it to him? He should just mind his own business. Someone around here is always nagging, and a person can't do anything without someone saying something about it. I am so annoyed that I am about to give him a fresh answer right then and there. Just in time I remember my charcoal makeup, and I slip past him without a word, with my head down. I had really better be careful. Fortunately the sky is overcast today; people would be able to notice my trick much more easily in the sunshine.

Two houses along I stop by the fence in amazement. The dog is outside, for the first time. I don't understand it. He isn't big or black at all or even the least bit scary. On the contrary. He stands no higher than my knees and is light brown. That's how wrong a person can be. I could never just say "Sic 'em!" to him and expect that he would bite everyone immediately. No one would be afraid of him. Maybe the people have two dogs? He even comes right up to the fence, wagging his tail at me in a friendly way. I hold my hand out to him and he licks it with his long, wet tongue. A nice little lap-dog, nothing wrong with that. Nevertheless, I am disappointed as I go on.

My place at the butcher's is free. From inside the store comes the shrill voice, "What'll it be, then?" I lean against the wall by the entrance.

My trick with the pitiful look works. It really works beyond all expectation. The very second woman says, "Wait a minute," and digs around in her shopping bag. I keep my head down so that the charcoal won't show. She presses something between my fingers and the collecting box, which has gotten so heavy meanwhile that I keep losing my grip on it.

A bar of chocolate. A whole bar of milk chocolate! It is really hard for me to keep a casual face. I would rather leap into the air for joy. I would rather hug the woman. A whole bar of chocolate! That's already something like a prize! And then she even puts some money in my collecting box.

I follow the woman with my eyes. She is quite fat and has on a brown skirt and a white blouse. The blouse strains over her back; you can clearly see where her bra is cutting in. She has big fat rolls of bacon. Then she turns around to me once. Now she's so far away that she certainly can't see the charcoal lines under my eyes anymore. I press the box to my stomach with my left hand, and with the right, in which I'm holding the chocolate, I wave to her and call, "God reward you!" the way the old women do. She laughs and waves back.

I quickly shove the chocolate into the pocket of my green windbreaker and look for my next victim.

It's people's own fault if they are so stupid. Huckleberry Finn would have liked the charcoal idea very much, I'm sure of that, but I doubt it would have occurred to him. And he never had to collect, either—he found a real treasure. And how cleverly he saved the money from his father! His dad would have drunk it all up on the spot.

An old woman comes out of the bakery; now there are no more customers inside. A good opportunity to beg for a roll.

Quickly I push the door open. A quite plump younger

woman is sitting on a stool behind the counter. She looks pleasant. She has her arms resting on the counter, and in front of her, right beside the cash register, stands a large jar of wafer cookies. The meringue fillings are pink, yellow, and light green, just like the ones in the bakery next to the building where my mother lives. Or used to. Perhaps she's moved now, I don't know. On the other side of the counter is a big plate heaped with coffee pastries, cinnamon buns, and croissants. They are covered with white frosting, and around the edges, where the frosting is very thin, I can clearly make out little lumps. Raisins.

Inside the shop it smells so wonderfully of bread and cake. Outside I didn't notice it at all. But in the first place, the bakery's door is always shut, unlike the butcher's, and in the second place, the stronger, smoky smell of sausage easily overwhelms the much more delicate bread smell. At least that's so with my nose, to which nothing smells stronger than sausage.

"What do you want?" asks the woman behind the counter as she stands up.

I lift my box and reach it toward her.

She waves it away. "Someone collected from us at our apartment door yesterday, and I don't donate more than once."

By her voice I realize that I was wrong. She is not pleasant. But I'm not about to give up so fast. I remain standing there and stare past her to the shelves on the back wall of the shop. Bread loaves of all sizes, and a case with rolls. Water rolls and French rolls, which have a groove down the middle.

The woman follows my look and her face turns angry. "Is there something else?" she asks. "Go now. I don't want you here collecting in the shop and annoying my customers."

Inside I murmur a curse, but I don't trust myself to say anything out loud. Then I go out again. Without a roll and without a wafer cookie. Of course I most want a pastry, with raisins and white frosting. But it's no good. Someone who has a cold heart will hide something rather than give it away. She can just choke on her stinginess!

My disappointment doesn't last long, though. How can it! I have a whole bar of chocolate in my pocket, and besides, I'm standing in front of the shop of the butcher lady with the two voices. "Come by again tomorrow," she said, and it sounded as though she really meant it.

With the chocolate in my pocket, the smell of sausage is almost bearable. All the same, I don't manage to hold out as long as I did yesterday, which anyway would not

have been very smart. "When good fortune comes call-
ing, open the door," Aunt Lou always says. When the
shadow of the building opposite has just reached the
middle of the street, I wait until there are no more customers in the store, and then I go inside.

I hold my box out to the woman, just like yesterday,
and then I drop my head as a precaution. The counter
isn't very wide, and I don't know if she might be able to
see the charcoal under my eyes or not. Besides, a lowered
head looks humble, and all adults like humble children
better than brazen ones.

"Here you are again," she says right away in her second voice, the gentle one, and holds something out to
me. A wienerwurst, I determine with a slanting glance
upward. No, two! I grab at them as fast as I can with my
head lowered. Today I am able to say immediately,
"Thank you." You can get used to anything, even something good. Once again her hand appears, this time with
a coin, a one-mark piece, which she drops in the slot of
my collecting box. A whole mark! I wish her a long and
healthy life with all my heart; she must really be a good
person.

Then once again I am standing in front of the shop.
Between one good donor and the next I sometimes take a

little bite of sausage. One is almost gone. That's too fast; I have to be more careful with it. I will wait for two more coin rattles until I can let myself have another bite. It's like a game and I am enjoying it. What a wonderful day.

In the building opposite, on the floor above the clothing store, an old woman is sitting at the open window. She supports herself on her elbows on the windowsill and looks over at me. Her cheeks are sunken in—certainly she has no teeth anymore. That reminds me that I must pull in my cheeks again. Another reason not to eat the sausage too fast; I'll wait for four contributions each time.

The first is a woman with a hat on her head, one of those small white things with a shimmering blue-green feather. A lady. Her nails are lacquered bright red. She puts three pieces of money into the slot. I never see them but I think they are only pennies because they don't clatter particularly loudly.

The next one is a man with a fat stomach and a double chin. I first have to tell him the entire story about Frau Heuss-Knapp, the good, kind, charitable wife of our president who founded the Mothers' Convalescent League. He listens to it all and even asks questions.

"Are the Amis involved?"

I have no idea if the Americans are involved, but just the way he says the word "Amis," I say quickly, "No."

"The Communists?" he asks, and his double chin quivers as he speaks. "Does it have anything to do with the Communists?"

"No," I say, although I have no idea who else besides Frau Heuss-Knapp is involved. "It's entirely a German thing."

Now it would have been good if I had long blond braids and not such straggly black hair. But he doesn't seem to be disturbed by that. He pokes a couple of coins into the box, and I imagine they sound like silver. Bigger coins sound different from pennies, that I have learned for sure in the meantime, even when the people often hold the money so that I can't see what they are putting in. Too bad the box isn't made of glass. That would have been much more exciting. Besides, then you could even let it drop by mistake. Of course not here on the street, where just anyone could pick up some of the money.

The third is another lady with a very neatly dressed child, a boy. Although he isn't much smaller than I am, she is still leading him by the hand. That just drives me crazy. I wouldn't want anyone to hold my hand at all on the open street, I think, and in spite of myself, tears of rage come into my eyes every time I see such a thing. It's especially bad when it's a child walking between a father and mother and being held by a hand on each side. I could murder such children. Or the mother, or the father—I'm not sure which. I only know that things like that make me furious.

Surreptitiously I run my hand over my blouse. The letter rustles slightly, and if I move I can feel it on my skin. Then I close my eyes for a moment and imagine Aunt Lou's face. My anger leaves me. When I think about Aunt Lou, I simply cannot stay angry. But I mustn't think about her too long, otherwise . . .

I open my eyes again. They still burn a little, but that could also be the sun, which has suddenly emerged from between two clouds and is blinding me.

Luckily the next contributor is not a woman with a child but one with two shopping bags, which she patiently sets down. Of course she gives me something. I look so pitiful today that no one can resist me. I can't be beaten; today I get everything I want. Only, no ten marks so that I can go see Aunt Lou.

All at once the bar of chocolate isn't so important. "When there is bitterness in the heart, sugar in the mouth doesn't help." That's also one of Aunt Lou's sayings.

I force myself not to think about her anymore, only

about collecting. For me it isn't a matter of the Mothers' Convalescent League. Why should I collect for mothers I don't know? It is a matter of the prize, which I intend to have. I take a big bite of the second wiener. But that doesn't taste as good to me as before, either. And the sun has disappeared behind the clouds again.

Toward five, my box has gotten very, very heavy. It must really be almost full. When I shake it, it only rattles dully, and when someone puts a coin in, it clinks against the others immediately. The box hasn't really rattled for a long time. There certainly must be quite a lot of money in there. I can't even begin to imagine what a person could do with it all. I had better think about the prize. It is surely mine, I think.

But will I really want it? Even if it's a book? Certainly it's a book, what else would it be? At the home, the girl in the graduating class who has the best grades always gets a book, Duro said. Usually an encyclopedia or the sayings from the classical age. A book isn't a bad prize.

But Aunt Lou's saying about the fat goose simply will not leave my head. I keep having to think about it even if I don't want to. I am so lost in thought that I don't notice anything at all on the way home. Suddenly there I am, standing at the gate.

Upstairs I rush to the bathroom and wash away the charcoal lines. I don't under any circumstances want the others to catch on to my trick. Of course, the collecting is over now, but who knows if I might not be able to use it again sometime.

*when the
thoughts are dark,
there can be
no light
in the heart*

I take off my bedspread. While I am carefully folding it up, I try not to look over at my collecting box on the night table. I don't succeed. My glance keeps snagging on the box. It's standing there, beside *Huckleberry Finn*. It's bright red, and it's jeering at me.

Huckleberry Finn wouldn't think about it as much as I do. But of course he's only in a book. In real life, things are a bit different, I think. For instance, Huckleberry Finn has a father who beats him when he's sober. That's not how it works, so I guess the man who wrote the book didn't know his stuff. In real life, parents beat their children when they are drunk, and when they are sober they hardly look at them.

And then this thing about how Huckleberry Finn runs

away from his father because he tries to kill him with a knife when he's boozing. That is described in such a funny way that I could laugh about it if I didn't know what something like that is in reality. Besides, each time I come to that place I feel sorry about the lovely pig. You see, Huckleberry Finn kills a pig just because he wants to leave a bloody trail to the river so that everyone will think he drowned. A whole pig just for a trail of blood, imagine that! All that meat—we could fill ourselves up on that for a whole week. He might have used something else. A rat, for instance—or maybe two, if there wouldn't be enough blood. Oh well, Huckleberry Finn just never lived in a home.

And he can always go into the woods when he wants to think, or to experience some kind of adventure. I often dream of that. Of woods and caves and of secret treasures and rafts on the river. I imagine myself catching fish with Huckleberry Finn and how we make a fire to cook them. The moon rises over the river and above it millions of stars in a sky like black velvet. Huck tells stories about ghosts and how you can protect yourself against them, and I laugh at him because he is such a scaredy-cat.

We do go walking in the forest on Sundays sometimes. But then there are always a lot of us. There are always a lot of us no matter what we do. And our forest is certainly not as large as Huckleberry Finn's woods are. But then he doesn't live here; he lives in America, on a great river called the Mississippi. When we came from Poland, my mother, Aunt Lou, and I, we also rode in a boat over a big river. Of course I can't remember it very clearly anymore, and of course it was night, but I'm sure that our river wasn't as beautiful as the Mississippi.

Perhaps everything is different in America. I must talk to Uncle Sam Silver about that sometime.

Dorothea puts her treasure box aside, takes my box in her hand, and weighs it. "Heavy," she says, "very heavy. You've collected a lot."

I nod and hang my folded bedspread over the back of the chair.

"I think you're going to win the prize," Dorothea says. "Elisabeth's box is nowhere near as heavy."

"It's not a matter of how heavy the box is," Elisabeth says haughtily. "It's what kind of coins are inside."

Across the way Susanne whispers something to Rosemarie, and Rosemarie laughs. Is it about me? Today I saw her together with Duro again.

Dorothea sits on her bed in her thin white nightgown with the bright blue borders, the cord with the key to her treasure box bouncing on her chest. She's already plaited her long hair into braids for the night. During the day she wears her hair down, to hide her hump, I think. Now you can see it very clearly.

Certainly she would have collected much more than me, because everyone would feel sorry for her. But she would never collect, because you have to go out on the street to do it, and she only does that when she absolutely has to. "I hate it when people stare at me," she often says. Yet she has a beautiful face with very bright gray eyes. In her white nightgown she almost looks like an angel. A slightly damaged angel, whose wings are broken off. Only the stump is still left.

I shrug and try not to look over. I don't want to see the box. I don't want to think about the box. But the rattling of the coins can't be overlooked, even though it sounds very dull. The goose has been well fed.

"No wonder you have so much," Elisabeth says from her place by the window. "Gypsies have begging in their blood."

For a moment everything swims before my eyes, but I say nothing. In the old days I used to have attacks of crying and throwing things, but that's long past. I've found a good trick: I just think of something entirely different. For instance, the red blouse I just took off. Aunt Lou bought it for me during the Easter vacation. I remember again how happy I was and think: Aunt Lou bought me a red blouse, so I can easily not listen to Elisabeth's stupid talk.

Besides this blouse I have only an old blue one from the home. The red one badly needs washing. Until yesterday, until I opened the letter from Aunt Lou, I was almost convinced that I would be going to her for the weekend. Then she would have washed my things. She always does. She gives me something old of hers to wear and washes everything I've brought with me. Here in the home we have our own laundry, but none of us puts our good things in it because so often something disappears. Only underclothes and nighties and stuff like that. Anyhow, I wouldn't let them wash my red blouse. We can also get soap powder from Frau Breitkopf and wash our own things. But I don't dare do that. In the winter I ruined a pullover that Aunt Lou knitted for me. It was pink with a border of gray cats. After I washed it, it was hard and much too tight. I cried for a week until Aunt Lou gave me a new one, but it wasn't nearly so pretty. Simply stripes made of leftover yarn.

I just got my underwear back from the laundry three days ago, and earlier this evening I quickly slipped the bar of chocolate under the pile, where it will be safe. I share my wardrobe with Renata, who is guaranteed not to go in there. She doesn't go burrowing around secretly in other people's things. I think that with her you could even just leave chocolate on the table and go out of the room, and when you came back it would still be there.

Unobtrusively I take Aunt Lou's letter out of my undershirt and shove it under my pillow. Tomorrow I will put it back inside my undershirt. First of all, I don't want it to fall into anyone else's hands—Elisabeth's, for instance—and second of all, I like to feel it when I walk around. Very much. It's almost as if Aunt Lou is soothing me.

Dorothea puts the box back on my night table. I hear it by the sharp clack of the metal on the wood. I pull a nightie, which also desperately needs washing, over my head and slip under my covers.

Scarcely a minute later Fräulein Urban comes and turns out the light.

Dorothea hasn't put her treasure box back in the cupboard but keeps it in bed with her. I think she always does that when she is very sad. Perhaps she's thinking about the prize and regretting that she didn't go collecting too. She's a strange girl, and I don't know if that's only on account of her hunched back. She has never said a word about her family, about before. No one knows anything about her, I think, not even whether she came here from another home or from her own.

Outside the dog is barking again. Very softly and very far away. The people must have another dog besides the little one that I saw. He couldn't possibly bark so loud that we could hear it all the way over here. Mine is large and black and walks like a lone wolf through the snowy forests. There are wolves in Poland, Aunt Lou says. They come over from Russia. I am afraid of wolves. But I would like a big dog. One who'd jump when I said, "Sic 'em!" A dog like that would be even better than cudgel-out-of-the-sack.

Now he's stopped barking.

I feel strange, almost as if I'm floating, and yet my arms and legs are stiff and trembling. My head feels swollen, and my throat is thick. I'm hot. Especially on the right side, where my night table is. The red box seems to glow like an oven; I can feel the heat on my face. Red rings dance before my eyes.

Aunt Lou says that people are good by nature. Only life makes them bad, the circumstances. I don't believe that. The circumstances here in the home are the same for all of us, and nevertheless some are bad and some aren't. Who could equate Elisabeth and Renata with each other? Yet they both live here, in the same room even. I would prefer not to think about myself. I think I'm not as good as Aunt Lou believes I am.

Susanne has already been tossing back and forth for quite a while, and now her movements grow slower and less forceful. Now Renata begins to cry. I open my eyes. At first I see nothing, but then my eyes get used to the gloom in the room, and I can clearly see the outlines of the box on my night table. Not its color, of course. Red quickly turns to black when it's dark. Like blood, when it clots.

What will be the prize that this local representative is providing? Naturally I'll see it, if one of us gets it. But perhaps there are other children collecting, too, from other schools, ones not connected with a home. I don't know. Fräulein Urban didn't say anything about it. But even if that's so, somehow I am sure that only one of us can win the prize, one of us home children. It must be so because we're the ones who really need it. The others already have everything, after all. Perhaps not everything they want, but they have parents, and they have things of their own. It isn't only from books that I know this; we see it all around us. After all, lots of children who aren't in the home go to school with us. They are called external students, in contrast to us. And we see them when we have outings and are allowed to go walking in the city. They play on the street or on bomb-damaged sites, or they go shopping with their mothers. Also some children ride their bicycles back and forth past the home and stare curiously in when we are down in the court-yard or on the playing field. They have terrific new bicy-cles. All right, I won't exaggerate, some also have very old bikes, but many do have new, shiny bikes in red, blue, or silver.

I don't even know how to ride a bike. Aunt Lou had one for a while, a very rickety one, and she wanted to teach me. But then I was suddenly taken to the sanato-rium, from one day to the next, and soon after that her bicycle finally collapsed. If she ever gets hold of another one, then I can learn on it, she promised me that.

Aunt Lou once told me a story, from earlier, from Poland, when she was still a child herself.

She had secretly taken her father's bicycle, put her lit-tle sister in front of her on the handlebars, and ridden off. Not far from the house where they were living, the road went downhill very steeply. "Very steep," Aunt Lou said. "A real abyss."

So she rode down the slope with her little sister and suddenly realized that she couldn't brake. She said the brakes were kaputt. I don't know if that's right; I have no idea how the brakes on a bike work. The bike went faster and faster, Aunt Lou said, and she was deathly afraid because the thing wouldn't stop. But her little sister thought it was fun.

Almost at the bottom of the street, Aunt Lou had three choices: the first, to just keep on riding onto the main road, but then a car or a truck could have been coming. Or maybe just a pedestrian, but that would have been bad enough. Or, second, she could have ridden into a tree that stood between the sloping street and the main road; or, third, into the thick shrubbery that surrounded the garden of Dr. Liepman. Naturally she chose the shrubbery, which I would have done too. Well, in the end the bike got all bent up, and her little sister had a cut on her head and skinned knees and elbows. What happened to Aunt Lou herself she didn't tell me. Only that her father walloped her.

"Not because of the bicycle," she said, "but because of my little sister, because I'd put her in danger. She could have been killed, he said. He was a good man, my father, but he had a hard hand."

That's something I don't understand. A man who has a hard hand can't also be a good man. Aunt Lou is sometimes very gullible; she finds an excuse for everything. I am completely the opposite. Anyway, I don't believe that my grandfather was as good a man as Aunt Lou thinks. He was killed, she said. Where and how I don't know, she always brushes that off. But he was supposed to have been a good man. Each time she speaks of him, she can't help crying.

She has never said anything about my grandmother. But, then, I never ask about before either, I wait until she brings it up herself. Somehow I don't want to ask. Maybe because she cries so easily.

By the way, Aunt Lou's little sister later became my mother. Sometimes I've considered what would have happened if Aunt Lou's adventure with the bicycle had ended differently. Her father—therefore my grandfather— did say, after all, that my mother could have been killed in that accident. And then what? Then there wouldn't have been any me. I can't imagine that. And, besides, Aunt Lou could have died too. I can imagine that even less. A world without Aunt Lou? Without her laugh? Without her sayings?

At the very thought, I feel as though my breath has been taken away. As if someone were forcefully holding my head under water.

Aunt Lou, you are right. When the thoughts are dark, there can be no light in the heart. Do you really never have dark thoughts?

only he
who bends to
pick up the coin
can put it
in his pocket

*E*lisabeth is snoring over by the window. Susanne is already asleep; also Dorothea; Jutta certainly; and even Renata has finally stopped crying and is breathing very quietly. Only Rosemarie might still be awake. I decide to wait a little longer. Suddenly I hear a bed creak and carefully peer under my half-open eyelids. Rosemarie. She gets up softly and slips out of the room. She hasn't even looked over at my bed once. Good, now I know, she's going to Duro. She should, then, if that fat cow pleases her better. I don't care at all. I can't stand either one of them.

Now I'm the only one still awake. I am glowing, and my collecting box is glowing too. It's gotten lighter in the room. Perhaps the moon has come out from behind a cloud. Anyhow, in the dusky light I can see Renata clearly. Her bed is next to the window, opposite Elisabeth's. Renata lies curled up on her side. With her right hand she has the tip of her blanket gathered up and pressed firmly against her mouth. She looks like a little child. Suddenly I think of Dolly; that was the way Dolly slept. Dolly from the other home, with whom I played so often. I can't remember at all anymore what her real name is; everyone called her Dolly. I wonder how she is. Strange that I haven't given a thought to her all this time. No, not strange, typical. I am simply very forgetful. When Susanne goes to see her sister the next time, I must send something to Dolly. I really must.

I get up softly and carefully and slip on my socks. My schoolbag creaks when I open it. Stupid, I should have taken out the pocketknife ahead of time. There it is. I slip into my green windbreaker because it's still cool at night, put the pocketknife in the pocket, and pick up the collecting box. Of course it isn't really glowing, I was just imagining it. It feels cold. To keep the money from rattling, I press it to my chest under the jacket and tiptoe to the door, then through the corridor to the handicrafts room, and to the luggage storeroom.

At last I am sitting on my koldra, in front of a burning candle, and holding the collecting box close to the light.

You can hardly see the two wires over the lead seal, really only their shadow on the red metal. Now, in the candlelight, it is the color of blooming poppies.

Maybe the prize is a bicycle?

No, I don't think so; a bike is much too expensive. Besides, the prize doesn't matter to me, or almost doesn't. I want something else. I want to go see Aunt Lou.

Of course, you aren't supposed to do what I am planning to. But so what? There are so many things a person isn't supposed to do.

"Only he who bends to pick up the coin can put it in his pocket," Aunt Lou says. That's the way it is. I am planning to bend.

Besides, if I take out ten marks for myself, then that's a lot of money for me, but for the Mothers' Convalescent League it's only a drop in the bucket. Perhaps a millimeter less butter on the bread. That won't be so bad. The mothers can stand it if they don't have butter spread as thick as your finger every day they are there.

In the home lots of things get swiped. Money and candy, for instance—things like that disappear like lightning if you don't watch out. And then there are all the things that you can't tell right off who they belong to, like watercolors, writing paper, things like that. We all scratch some kind of a sign on the side of our pencils.

However, other things are safer. Never in their lives would anyone steal Elisabeth's doll or even my bedspread, for instance. Anyway, what could you do with any of those things? Everybody would recognize them.

I don't really find stealing so bad. But Aunt Lou says there is a difference between mine and yours. The only time it's somewhat different is when someone is very, very hungry. Stealing still isn't right then either, she says, but you can understand it. But, Aunt Lou, if someone has a longing, that's something like hunger, isn't it? Wouldn't you say that longing . . . that's when the soul is hungry?

And besides, I just won't tell her; I will say I just happened to find a ten-mark note on the street. Of course I don't like to lie to her, but if the truth is going to make her sad, it's better for her to just not find it out.

I have an entirely different worry. What will happen if it comes out? What will happen if they see that I broke the wire? Fine. Then I just say, "It was an accident. I was playing around with it and the wire got broken by mistake. It's so thin, after all." And if they keep on asking, "Why didn't you tell Fräulein Urban right away?" then I can say, "I was afraid that you would think I took something. But I didn't. I didn't take anything."

If I just stay firm, they can't do anything to me. How

can they prove I've taken anything? Nobody can know how much people really put into my box.

But I have to hide the money in case anyone looks for it. Behind the beam, yes, that's a good idea. "You just have to stick to your story and make sure they don't find any evidence," Arnulf always said. Arnulf lived in the house next door when I was still with my mother. He was often picked up by the police. He was the best black marketeer of all the children. No one ever found out where and how he got hold of the American ciga-rettes. He never told. The police always had to let him go again. Arnulf was clever and cunning, he managed everything. By the way, he was also the one who gave me the pocketknife that time I had to go to the sanatorium. "For a going-away present and a keepsake," he said. Yet he couldn't have had any idea then that we wouldn't see each other again. I didn't know myself that I wouldn't be coming back to my mother.

But at the sanatorium they saw my back and my legs, and then the lady from Welfare came and took charge of everything. "You don't need to be afraid anymore," she said. She didn't understand anything, but she tried. Aunt Lou just about exploded when she heard the word *home*. She simply cannot hide her feelings. I was like that once, too, but in the meantime I've learned a lot. You don't let anything show and you never say what you really think. And you even have to be careful when it comes to thinking. There are thoughts you have to protect yourself from.

I pull the box away from the candle so that the paint won't get singed and get little bubbles that then won't smooth away again. It has a thin wire passed through a tiny tube in the clasp of the cover, and then both ends of that are threaded through a little loop on the box's upper edge and welded together—or whatever you call it—with a lead seal. The distance between the little tube and the loop is very small, and I just cannot find anyplace where I can get the knife in properly to cut through one of the two parts of the wire. I fiddle and fumble, but I keep having to be careful not to let the blade slip and, God forbid, make a scratch in the red lacquer.

It simply won't work. The wire is too tight against the box. A pocketknife isn't the right tool for such a job. I fold it up and put it in my jacket pocket. I think of the scissors on the shelves outside. I stand up and listen at the door for any suspicious noises before I unlock it.

Although no one ever comes into the handicrafts room at night, I am never completely free of fear. But I'm not

afraid of spirits or ghosts prowling in the quiet home at
night—though Huckleberry Finn certainly would be—
just of Fräulein Urban. I imagine her suddenly opening
the door and asking, "What are you doing in here at this
hour?" That would be especially bad tonight, but I
wouldn't know what to answer anyhow. As far as that
goes, I'm less afraid of the punishment, even if it's dishwashing duty, than that the key to the luggage storeroom won't be left in the box anymore. By the light of
the candle I pick out a couple of pairs of scissors and take
them with me. I'll leave one of them behind the beam
later; you never know when you might need it again.

It works right away with the first one, a narrow,
pointed pair. The wire can be cut through quite easily,
more easily than I thought. I do make a small scratch in
the box, though, but no one will notice that. I push the
wire through the little tube, then fold back the cover.
The box is full, almost up to the edges. Certainly I have
won the prize. There could hardly be more in any box
other than mine. But that doesn't matter to me now. I
don't need the stupid prize.

I root around in the money for a bit. The coins feel
thick and clank softly. I feel very funny at the sight of so
much money. Of course there are a lot of pfennigs and
two-pfennig coins in there, but most are tens and fives.

Every now and then there is also a little bit of silver. This won't be enough just for the Mothers' Convalescent League, it will be enough for me, too. I reach in and lay a handful of coins on the koldra, then another, then another. Finally there is a whole mountain of money in front of me. So much! What a person could do with all that!

What if I say the box was stolen from me? Some strange man snatched it out of my hand? No, you can forget that—they'd never believe me. Or that I left it behind somewhere by mistake. I can just banish such thoughts from my head right now.

But I am still a little sad about all that money. There are ten fifty-pfennig pieces in there, three marks, and even a two-mark piece. That is certainly from the woman in the butcher shop, the first time, when I looked at the sausage. I take the two-mark piece, a one-mark piece, and six fifty-pfennig coins. Then I count out forty ten-pfennig coins. I wrap the entire little pile up in a piece of newspaper and immediately hide it behind the beam, back in the farthest corner.

Then I put the other coins back into the box again, carefully, almost one by one, because suddenly every tiny clink and clatter sounds like thunder to me.

Anyhow, now I feel sick. Not because I've stolen. What

does *stolen* mean? I haven't stolen. I've taken something for myself that the box has more than enough of. And I need the money. I have to go to see Aunt Lou. No matter what. Otherwise I will get sick again. I'm already feeling sick to my stomach. Tomorrow is Saturday. Tomorrow I will go to see Aunt Lou. I will tell Fräulein Urban just at the last moment, after school, just before I have to go to the train station. Then she can't do anything more about it. On Saturdays you can't call Aunt Lou, either. Certainly she will let me go. Tomorrow . . .

But then I think: you shouldn't be too brazen, even when you are taking what you are entitled to. Otherwise the thing might turn out badly. All right. I won't go to Aunt Lou tomorrow, I'll wait until next week.

Now I feel a little better. Then it occurs to me that I should give Renata the chocolate. Not as a punishment for me, but as a balance, so that I won't get too much. May the hands of those who never give become empty. Today at supper Inge secretly pressed a candy into my hand, a caramel. Only me, not the others. I'll give Renata the chocolate so that she has something too. That's a good decision, and suddenly I feel much better.

All I have to do now is push the wire through the little tube and carefully twist the two ends together so that no one can see that I've undone them.

And suddenly—suddenly my breath stops. One thing I haven't thought of. Even if I pull ever so hard, the two ends of the wire just barely meet; there can be no thought of twisting them together. My hands begin to tremble. How could I have been so dumb? Why didn't I think of this before? I ought to have figured out where the extra wire I need is going to come from.

Calm, stay very calm, or it's all over with. I have to control myself and consider very calmly what I can do now. That shouldn't be difficult for me, I've already had to do it many times, I've had lots of practice.

Nevertheless it's some time before my hands stop trembling. And then a solution occurs to me: I'll fasten the two ends together with a drop of candle wax. When the wax dries, it will hold to some extent. Let's hope no one will pull on the seal.

But it isn't so easy. A real fiddly job, during which my hands must not tremble. I force myself to think of nothing, nothing at all, not even Aunt Lou. Especially not of Aunt Lou. Only of what I must do now.

I hold the box somewhat at an angle, slip a finger under the ends of the wire, and let the wax drop onto them. It's hot, I jump, and a little drop falls on the box. While the wax is hardening, I carefully scratch off the stiffened droplet with my fingernail.

The stuff takes a nice long time until it is dry and hard. At first it looks as though it has worked, the wires are together. But when I try to make the little roll of wax a bit narrower, it immediately crumbles and the ends of the wire snap apart.

So I have to do the whole process over again. I mustn't use as much wax as I did the first time and also have to roll it a little thinner.

But it doesn't work the second time either.

I should never have begun the whole thing! But now it's too late.

I go into the handicrafts room with the candle, put back the scissors, and look for something I can use. I am lucky. In a drawer of craft stuff I find a tube of Uhu cement. That will have to work.

This time I'm more careful. I tip the collecting box on its side, grasping it between my knees so that the cover won't be pushed open by the coins, slip two fingers under the ends of the wire, and hold them together. Then I carefully squeeze a drop of cement on it. There. And now slowly withdrawing my hand, I shove up the seal from underneath, press the wire into the little tube, and wait for the cement to dry.

Wait, wait, wait. And don't think of anything, anything at all.

I don't know how long it takes, a few minutes or an hour. I sit frozen. Then I try to see if it has worked. Yes. The little lump has even stretched a little. Only it's too light and so transparent that you immediately see the two ends of the wire, which do not meet. But that's no big problem. With some spit and dust from the floor I color the little roll of cement light gray and also smear the box around the seal a little so that it looks slightly dirty but not damaged.

If people don't look closely—and why should anyone?—it all seems quite normal. A little dirty, but otherwise unremarkable.

I put the box on the koldra. The candle flickers in the draft that's coming through the cracks between the roof tiles. Now I really begin to shake. And I can't help crying with relief.

Once I've actually begun crying, I can't stop very easily, I know that. I pick up my Pelikan Oil bottle and take off the cover. But it doesn't help. I have to keep on crying until my head is thundering and my throat is sore with sobbing.

But sometime or other it's finally over. Now just a little whiff, to calm down. My head is completely empty.

Then I carefully carry the box back and put it on my night table so that the dirty spot isn't facing the room.

Rosemarie is back in her bed and asleep. Has she seen that I wasn't here? Where would she think I was? But that doesn't bother me. She'd never tell Fräulein Urban that I wasn't in the room tonight. If she does, I'll tell that she left after lights-out. However, I don't really think she will snitch, that's not her style. No matter. Nothing matters.

Finally I am lying in bed, and I am thinking about Dolly.

I see her face before me, her thin arms. How could I ever have forgotten her? At that time I so wished that she could be my little sister. Someone to love. How are things going for her now? Has she found another big girl to protect her?

Dolly sometimes sang us a song, "O Congaserro," or something like that—anyhow, it wasn't a German song. And then she turned in a circle and lifted her skirt so high that you could see her underpants. I thought it was really sweet the way she did it. But once Frau Maurer came in and got very excited and yelled that Dolly "must never, never do that." Her face was white with rage, and she very seldom yelled either. Dolly began to cry. And then Frau Maurer took her in her arms and kissed her. But Dolly didn't want to be kissed by Frau Maurer, she kept on crying, and she didn't stop until I

comforted her. Frau Maurer never objected to Dolly's
sleeping with me after that. I do not know to this day
why that was all so strange. Dolly was afraid, and I was
afraid too.

Why can't I think of something more cheerful now? I
ought to be glad that I have the money for train fare. I
really ought to be able to go to sleep calmly now.

I begin to count. I count five- and ten-pfennig pieces,
and sometimes there is the shimmer of silver. My fingertips are sore from the hot wax. And what's more, I stuck
myself in the tip of my right index finger with the
scissors.

Suddenly I remember Dolly's real name: Sigrid.

even in the
garden of eden
it wouldn't
be good
to be alone

next morning at breakfast, Fräulein Urban stands up and swings her brass bell. She says she wants to collect the boxes for the Mothers' Convalescent League right after breakfast. All the collectors should come to the handicrafts room and hand in their boxes before school begins.

All of a sudden I'm not hungry anymore and put the second slice of bread that I already have in my hand back in the basket. There is still half my portion of margarine on my plate. I lift it with my knife and hold it out to Renata. But she shakes her head. She doesn't want my margarine; obviously she isn't hungry.

"Give it here," says Duro, and she stretches out her

hand. There's nothing else for me to do but give her the margarine, the fat cow.

"What's the matter, Halinka, are you getting sick again?" Inge asks from the other end of the table. I shrug. It could well be that I am getting sick. Anyway, I do feel a little sick to my stomach.

"I have infirmary duty starting today," Inge says.

With weak knees I climb the stairs. First I go to the toilet because I feel sick. I stand there bent over the toilet. I have to retch, but except for a little bit of mucus, nothing comes up.

Then I go to the room. Elisabeth is just getting her box and leaves right away. She is wearing her new brown top and has the green scarf tied around her neck. I reach for my box. Everything blurs before my eyes, and I can't even see the wire clearly anymore. Earlier, before breakfast, even in the bright light of morning, it looked very good, but now I am filled with doubts. What if Fräulein Urban sees it? What will I say?

I hold the box in such a way as not to touch the seal, for God's sake. My legs feel weak and my face is feverishly hot. To cool off, I go first to the washroom and wash my face.

Fräulein Urban is standing by the cutting table in the

handicrafts room, in front of her the cardboard cartons for the collecting boxes. This time there are only two cartons. Elfriede is leaning at the window. Elfriede is Fräulein Urban's pet, as every girl in the home knows. But I don't envy her. Fräulein Urban always calls her when she needs help. For instance, Fräulein Urban rarely goes through the corridor with the gong; usually Elfriede does it. And if there is something heavy to carry, of course she always has to help because she is so big and strong. It serves her right. I wonder if Fräulein Urban has any idea how often Elfriede hits people?

Fräulein Urban has made up labels with names, and she attaches them to the boxes. Elisabeth has already handed in hers, then comes Claudia and the new girl in the fifth grade. What is her name? I must ask Susanne later. Later, when I've gotten through this business.

"When does the winner get the prize?" Claudia asks.

Fräulein Urban takes the box out of her hand. "The prize will probably be awarded next Wednesday. And Frau Lehmann said that she would try to count all the money over the weekend. If all goes well, she'll know by Monday who the lucky one is."

So the local representative is named Frau Lehmann. For all I care, she can call herself whatever she wants to.

Now it's my turn. I shift my box so that Fräulein Urban can take it by the handle. She holds it in her hand for a moment, and suddenly I can't breathe. She hesitates, and my heart throbs all the way up to my eyes. Then she smiles broadly and puts the box into the carton, into the second one, which is now almost full. On top, on the cover, she sticks a label with my name on it.

"Your box is very heavy, Halinka," she says to me. "Really, very heavy."

I can breathe again, and suddenly nothing matters anymore. I shrug my shoulders indifferently. I have my prize already, I can't imagine a better one. Next weekend I will go to see Aunt Lou. It will be ten weeks then. I will go to see her, and nothing else matters to me. Nobody matters to me. Not Elfriede, not Fräulein Urban. Not even Rosemarie, or Renata, the dumb cow who refused my margarine. Renata is a stupid name, anyway, but I don't care about that either.

After lunch Jutta and Susanne pack their things. Jutta is going to her grandmother's and Susanne is going to Hildegardis to see her little sister. Then I have an idea: I will give Susanne something to take to Dolly. But I don't have anything, except for the chocolate, which I really want to give to Renata. Besides, I'm sure that

Susanne would eat the bar of chocolate herself on the way there. I run into the next room, to Inge, and ask if she could give me another caramel. She looks at me in astonishment.

"Susanne is going to Hildegardis, to her sister," I say. "I want to give her something to take to Dolly."

She understands immediately and gets three candies and a red lollipop out of her wardrobe. "Here," she says. "You might as well take them, I have enough." Inge is definitely not stingy.

I run back. Susanne hasn't left yet. Quickly I snatch a piece of paper from my drawing pad, draw a little doll on it, write greetings, and wrap the three caramels and the lollipop in the paper. Susanne takes the little packet and sticks it in her bag. "And tell Dolly she should write back to me, too," I say.

Susanne nods, takes her bag, and leaves, along with Jutta. They're taking the same train. This time I'm not even envious. They can go. Every one of them can, for all I care! I have something that I can be happy about.

Unfortunately it's raining. Otherwise I would go to the ball fields. On most Saturday afternoons some of the big kids are there playing dodgeball, and sometimes, if I'm lucky, they let me play with them. When there are so many that they don't need me, I practice broad jumping or something like that. But none of that happens when it rains. When it rains I have to stay inside.

But perhaps it's better this way. I really am feeling a little weak. No wonder; I didn't sleep much last night.

I look at the big clock in the corridor. It's five minutes past 2:30. If I were taking the 2:27 train, I would already have been under way for eight minutes. Instead of that, I'm here. Well, I'll just read a little. Or daydream. Rest, anyhow.

Rosemarie is sitting at her desk, with her drawing pad in front of her and her box of watercolors. She paints often, either pictures of flowers or beautiful ladies with long hair. Her ladies wear dresses with deep necklines and puffed sleeves. Sometimes they hold a fan, and often butterflies are flying around them. Last night Rosemarie was with Duro, and perhaps she knows that I know it. When she came back she must have seen that my bed was empty. On the other hand, maybe she didn't look over at my bed at all, since I matter so little to her.

Elisabeth is perched on her bed with her legs crossed, combing the hair of her stupid doll. Dorothea is sitting on her own bed, her back propped against the head end, her arms crossed behind her neck. You can't see her hump at all, only that her neck is a little bit short. She is playing "I see something you don't see" with Elisabeth.

I really am very tired. So I take off my shoes and lie down on my bed. I spend most of my free time on my bed anyhow. I'm not the only one to do that; almost all the others do too. Often we simply don't know what else to do.

I don't read; I pretend to sleep. I really enjoy it when Elisabeth and Dorothea play "I see something you don't see." I silently play along with them, without their knowing it.

However, my rules are different from the regular ones. While Elisabeth and Dorothea have to pick objects that are in the room, in my game the rule is that I have to select things that are not in the room but in my memory. And I have to describe them very precisely. That's much more difficult than you might imagine, and maybe that's the very reason why I find it so much fun.

"I see something you don't see, and it's yellow," Elisabeth says.

Yellow. Yellow was the wheat field, it was late summer then. I had gone out into the country with Aunt Lou. That was when she had the bicycle. She had come simply because she wanted to visit with us, me and my mother, but then she saw the strange man, and the black-and-blue marks on my arm, so she took me out for a bicycle ride. I sat on the hard luggage carrier and stuck my legs way out to the side so they wouldn't get caught in the spokes. When we came to the wheat field, we got off because it was so beautiful. Entirely yellow. Or no, it wasn't only yellow, there was also a little brown in the yellow. And a dash of green. And everywhere there were colorful spots of flowers. Red spots of field poppies and blue of cornflowers.

At the edge of the field there were other blue flowers whose blue was lighter than that of the cornflowers, and their leaves were a brighter green, somehow sandier. The flowers grew densely on the stem and were deeply cut. As if they were made of paper. As if someone had cut a circle out of paper and then cut in from the edge in small strips. I liked these flowers very much. I asked Aunt Lou what they were called, but she only knew the Polish name, which I've now forgotten. I wanted to pick some, but they were hard to break off, and the stem cut into the side of my hand when I pulled on it. I didn't yet have the knife that Arnulf gave me as a going-away present.

I think it was a few days later that the doctor with the X-ray van stopped at the schoolyard and examined us all—I don't remember exactly anymore. Anyhow, the day after the bike ride I showed the flower to my teacher and asked her what it was called. She said it was chicory, and they also call it "pathwatch" in German. A beautiful name. A flower that stands by the path and watches. For whom? For me, of course. In the sanatorium I often thought of this flower and imagined that it was standing there and watching for me to come back. But I didn't; I never saw it again.

"The notebook at Renata's place," Dorothea says.

"No," Elisabeth says triumphantly. "That's four wrong. You only get one more."

"I give up," Dorothea says.

Elisabeth laughs loudly. "Rosemarie's socks."

"But those are in her wardrobe," Dorothea protests. "You can't see those at all."

Elisabeth's voice is arrogant. "The rule is that you can use anything in the room. And you know as well as I do that Rosemarie has yellow socks."

Rosemarie grins. I dart a glance over at Dorothea. She's angry, but you can't fight Elisabeth. No one can. Dorothea presses her lips together so hard that they look white and stick out like an old, badly healed scar. "All right," she says, "but now it's my turn. I see something you don't see, and it's brown."

"My new top," says Elisabeth.

"No." Dorothea giggles.

"One of the desks," Elisabeth says. "Brown is a dumb color. There is so much brown."

"All the same," Dorothea says. "Besides, you're only allowed to say one desk each time. But I don't mind helping you—desks aren't it."

Brown. Brown is the color of the dress my mother was wearing when we were at the hearing. The lady from Welfare had me firmly by the hand. My mother didn't even look at me. Anyway, not at the beginning, when I saw her brown dress. I don't know if she ever looked at me later, because I was staring at the floor. The floor was also brown, with dark cracks and darker streaks in the grain. All I know for certain is that one of the streaks looked like a lizard.

"In Poland there are many lizards," Aunt Lou said when I told her. "In the summer they lie on hot stones, and when you catch them and hold them by their tails, their tails just fall off."

At first I felt sorry for the lizards, but then Aunt Lou said that they grew back a new tail. Practical. That doesn't happen with people. When you grab hold of a person too hard, she gets black-and-blue marks and big bruises, and everything hurts. But her arms never just fall off and then grow back again. Too bad. I would love to be a lizard and just lie on a hot stone in the sun. Preferably in the forest, in a clearing. The tree trunks in the forest are also brown, just like the old leaves that lie on the ground. And the underbrush, which always looks a little scary.

"My shoe," Elisabeth says.

"No." Dorothea's voice sounds pleased and a little bit spiteful. She must have hit on something very special. Brown is really a good color. Elisabeth doesn't have a chance. There are seven of us in the room, and we all have brown shoes.

"Your shoes?"

"No." Dorothea giggles. "You'll never guess."

"The Gypsy's eyes?"

"No! I win!" Dorothea jumps off the bed and points to a tiny spot on the wall under her night table. "Here— this flyspeck!"

"That's not fair," Elisabeth says. "From here it looks black."

"But it's brown," says Dorothea triumphantly. "Brown, brown, brown. As brown as brown poop when there have been brown beans for dinner."

And as brown as the chocolate that's lying in the wardrobe under my underwear. And like the chocolate I got from Uncle Sam Silver nine weeks ago.

Uncle is English and means the same as *Onkel* in German. Of course he isn't my uncle, but I'm allowed to call him "Uncle." He's Aunt Lou's boyfriend. At least I think he is. I didn't ask her, I don't dare. I know that Aunt Lou would very much like to get married, and not just because of me. "Even in the Garden of Eden it wouldn't be good to be alone," she said to me one time.

I understand about not wanting to be alone. Even Huckleberry Finn is very happy when he meets Miss Watson's Jim and can travel on with him. And maybe there on the Mississippi it looks like the Garden of Eden. But it certainly doesn't in Aunt Lou's furnished room. That's very small. After a wardrobe cupboard and a bed there's only room left for a table and a chair. And a sofa. I sleep on it when I'm visiting. No, really, I picture the Garden of Eden quite differently.

Aunt Lou works in an American canteen, from noon until late into the night. That's why she can't have me with her. My guardian—some person in an office I've never even met—denied her second petition too. The first time he said that I couldn't live with her because she had no regular job, and the second time that she couldn't take care of me because she worked until too late at night. "I can't do anything about it," Aunt Lou said that time, after she had cried a little first. "He can say where you are going to live; the court decided that. But when I find a man and marry, I'll go back again, you can count on that, and then he can't say anything more."

Since then I've hoped she would find a man. Therefore I looked over this Uncle Sam Silver very carefully. He's in the army. I like him very much. But whether he has money and if he even wants to marry, that of course I don't know. Aunt Lou has only known him for three or four months, and apparently marriage doesn't go that fast.

My mother never married, I think. Anyhow, in the class book where it says name of the father, for me there's a blank line. Damn, I don't want to think about my mother. Sometimes I really go for days or weeks without thinking of her. It's only happening to me so often since this collection for the Mothers' Convalescent League started.

Aunt Lou. Aunt Lou and Uncle Sam Silver. I mustn't hope for a miracle so that I won't be disappointed afterwards. But ever since I met Uncle Sam Silver, during the Easter vacation, I sometimes think of the small, tiny possibility. But only sometimes. There are also days when I think I will never get out of here. Simply never, never, never. Then I imagine how every year some leave, and every year new ones come in, and I am always still here. I will grow old and older, and finally I will die here in this room, on this bed, without ever having seen a single orchid.

*once a person
has bread,
he also finds
a knife*

I can't concentrate on counting. My head is in a muddle. This boring, rainy weekend isn't boring at all. Just the opposite. It isn't only bad luck that doesn't come singly; it happens with good luck too. Or, as Aunt Lou says, "Once a person has bread, he also finds a knife."

But from the beginning. My old trick: you lie on your back, close your eyes, and relive a nice thing all over again. You imagine how everything looked and what happened from the beginning. Every word, every movement, every color. This way you don't forget something nice so quickly, and you can have it twice, three times, four times, or five times over again. Then, by the sixth time it usually gets a little boring, because you really do get used to everything, even nice things.

I lie on my back, look up at the ceiling, which now, in the middle of the night, looks like a dark gray cloud; then I close my eyes and imagine it all from the beginning. . . .

It is Saturday night, a few hours ago. Elisabeth and Dorothea are already asleep; Jutta and Susanne aren't there; and Rosemarie has gone to her new friend Duro. Then Renata begins to cry. I try to think about something else, about orchids, for instance, and suddenly I think of the chocolate. I had intended to put it under Renata's pillow this afternoon, but at the last minute I couldn't stand the idea of losing all that lovely chocolate. Now, however, I feel sorry that I didn't give it to Renata. It's almost as if I hadn't kept a promise. Though I didn't make it out loud.

I stand up, get the chocolate out of the wardrobe, and sit on the edge of Renata's bed. I can clearly make out her head with its brown hair, it's so bright in here. The moon is almost full tonight, and there isn't a single cloud left in the sky. The rain has cleared up.

Renata of course notices that someone is sitting beside her, but she doesn't know that it's me. She doesn't lift her head, only tries to push me away with her elbow. She mumbles something I can't understand. But I am stubborn. She's going to eat the chocolate, damn it. She's going to eat it, and how! She's not going to stop me from doing something good now!

I carefully tear off the paper, although I don't need to be so quiet. Elisabeth and Dorothea are really deep sleepers, that I know for sure. I break off a piece of chocolate and try to shove it into Renata's mouth. She lifts her right arm a little higher to push me away, but I push my hand between her head and her arm. It's hard to find her mouth because she's buried her face in her hands. Everything is wet with tears and snot, so everything feels slippery and it's even harder to find her mouth. Finally I manage it, and the piece of chocolate is inside. At least I think so, because I'm careful not to push my finger in after it.

She stops crying—suddenly, like a little child when you stick the pacifier in its face. I saw that once when I was going to Aunt Lou's. On the train, a woman with a baby was sitting across from me. It was really funny: from one second to the next the baby stopped crying.

Like Renata. She turns over, sits up, and looks at me. I make an effort to smile in a very friendly way and shove the piece of chocolate—in her astonishment, it has half slipped out—back into her mouth. Even with the lights out I can see how messy her face is. I haven't managed this operation very skillfully.

Renata would have been really nice as a younger sister.

I stand up and pull her out of bed and along behind me to the washroom. There you can turn on the light without worrying, because you're supposed to wash your hands when you go to the bathroom. Fräulein Urban has a thing about hand washing. So I turn on the light and push Renata over to the mirror. She stares at it. There are two faces, hers and mine. I have to laugh because she looks so funny, and then she begins to laugh too. Her teeth look very white against the chocolate-smeared mouth. She washes her face, and I watch her. And then I suddenly have an idea.

"Let's go," I say. "Put your socks on very quietly and put your sweater on over your nightie and come with me. I'll show you something."

We get our socks and our sweaters, and I also take the opened bar of chocolate from the top of her bed. Without asking anything, Renata slips along the wall behind me. When I get the key to the luggage storeroom from the shelf, her eyes get huge. But she stays very quiet until we are sitting on the koldra behind the wall of suitcases. Then she says the first word: "Nice."

The candle burns, and we sit there and look at each

other. I had entirely forgotten how a face keeps changing when a candle flickers.

I can't think of anything to say. And Renata obviously can't either. Therefore I break off a piece of chocolate and stick it in her mouth. She takes the bar out of my hand, breaks off a piece, and sticks it in my mouth. So we sit for a long time, companionably sucking on chocolate.

"Where did you get the chocolate?" Renata asks suddenly.

I tell her about the woman in the brown skirt and white blouse.

"You collected a lot," she says. "Dorothea says that you're certainly going to win the prize. And Elisabeth is terribly angry and says mean things about you."

"I don't think that I will win the prize," I say though not a word about why I won't win it.

"If I had been that woman with the brown skirt and white blouse I'd also rather have given you something than Elisabeth."

I laugh. Renata laughs too.

"In the home where I was before," I said, "there was a little girl who slept just like you with the tip of the covers in front of her face. She was called Dolly, and I often wished she was my little sister."

"Funny," said Renata. "I never wished for a little sister, only a big one. A big sister who knew everything and helped me."

We look at each other. Suddenly there is something between us, something close. The candle flickers, and outside a dog barks. It's a different one, with a lighter voice, and the barking comes from the opposite direction.

"I had a friend at home," Renata says slowly. "As proof of our friendship, we told the worst thing that we had done recently. Something we were ashamed of."

I stare at her. I have never told anyone anything bad, not even Aunt Lou. No, especially not Aunt Lou. I wouldn't want to make her sad.

"Are you serious?" I ask.

She nods and shoves the last piece of chocolate into my mouth. She folds up the paper neatly and sticks it in her sweater pocket. That pleases me. Obviously she knows that you have to be careful if you don't want to get caught. Chocolate paper in the luggage storeroom would immediately make Fräulein Urban suspicious.

"If you tell a friend something that you are ashamed of, they can never be mean to you or tell on you," she says. "Because then you can tell on them too."

I understand that. Nevertheless, something about this idea disturbs me. Hesitantly I stand up and get my thoughts book. The light of the candle doesn't reach to the corner with the roof tile, but I find it even in the dark. After all, Renata doesn't have to know all my hiding places.

I sit down beside her, open my thoughts book, and read something to her that I wrote a few weeks ago. "A person has to be very careful about wishes. If you want something very, very badly, it may easily turn out to be something entirely different."

"I don't understand that," Renata says. "Why did you write that?"

She looks as if she really wants to know. "I was sick," I begin. "I'm often sick."

Then I stop. I don't like this telling. No one is supposed to know anything about me. That's why I only write memory cues in my thoughts book, not what really happened. When I read the cues, I remember everything, but nobody else understands. No, I never tell anything. Why should I make an exception this time? Renata is looking at me with big eyes. They look much darker than usual. Renata doesn't really look like Dolly. I lower my head.

"I was sick," I start over. "So I was lying there in the infirmary and knew for sure that no one would come for the whole morning. Because it was a Monday, and

Mondays Fräulein Urban teaches all six periods. I was bored; I happened not to have a book. The infirmary is hideous, and even in the sunlight it doesn't look any better. The three other beds were empty and just as white as mine. I looked at the yellow spots on the white metal bed frames and thought they looked as though someone had peed on them. And through the bedsheet I could feel the rubber sheet under my behind, in case I wet the bed. I haven't wet the bed for years.

"I considered what I could do. And all of a sudden I had an idea. Elisabeth's doll. I could play with Elisabeth's doll without worrying about a thing. I've never had a doll, I don't think, and meanwhile I've gotten too old for it. But I would like to have played with one once.

"So I sneaked into our room. Luckily I didn't meet anyone in the corridor. The room was empty—everybody else was in school—and the doll was sitting on Elisabeth's bed. I picked her up and looked her over very carefully and felt her blond hair. It isn't anywhere near so soft as it looks.

"I remember that I wondered whether all dolls have blond hair. Claudia's also has blond hair. Very long blond curls. Sometimes Claudia gives her braids, and sometimes she ties a blue ribbon in her hair. Blue ribbons in blond hair are very pretty. In black hair red are prettier, my aunt Lou said when she gave me a red ribbon one time, but I soon lost it. But that isn't part of this.

"So I sat there, on Elisabeth's bed, with the doll in my hand, and wanted to play with her. But I didn't know how. The doll just stared at me with her dumb blue eyes.

" 'You have mean eyes, just like Elisabeth,' I said to her.

"She didn't answer me. But when Elisabeth plays with her, she answers in a very high, squeaky voice. So I said it again, about the mean eyes.

" 'You're only jealous because you don't have beautiful blue eyes yourself,' she squeaked all at once. It wasn't at all easy to talk so high, it tickled my throat terribly.

" 'Blue eyes aren't beautiful at all,' I said to the stupid doll. 'My aunt Lou has very dark eyes, almost black. And my aunt Lou is the most beautiful woman in the world. Uncle Sam Silver said so.'

"The doll put on a snooty expression, just like Elisabeth. 'Your uncle Sam Silver is only an Ami soldier,' she said, 'and your aunt Lou is an Ami floozy.'

"And all of a sudden I knew how you play with dolls. I put her over my knee, pulled down her underpants, and spanked her until my hand hurt.

"And then suddenly I started to cry. I pulled up the dumb doll's pants again, smoothed her skirt, and put her back on Elisabeth's bed exactly the way she'd been before. And I kept thinking while I was doing it, good thing I didn't beat her to death. And then I went back to the infirmary again and was ashamed of myself.

"I remember what I thought, something really silly, which was, lucky that dolls don't get bruises and big black-and-blue marks, and lucky, too, that dolls don't cry."

I stop. Suddenly I don't think the story is so bad, only kind of foolish. But until now I've always gotten a stomachache when I think of how I beat the doll. Maybe it's different this time because I've told someone. But suddenly I am afraid again because now someone knows about it.

Why have I told Renata anything, anyhow? And why did I start? She should have gone first. After all, I showed her my hideout.

"I don't want to hear your story now," I say to her. "I want to go to bed."

Renata stands up immediately. She rolls up the koldra and pushes it deep under the slant of the roof. I carry the candle to the door, blow it out, and hide it behind the beam again. We get back to our room unseen.

I'm lying there and still I can't fall asleep. I don't think she's asleep either. So I can't even begin to count yet. I don't know if I am happy or not. Yes, I *am* happy, but I ought to have been more careful. One should never show too much of oneself.

I absolutely must write Dolly a letter. I must tell her that she should never sing "O Congaserro" again and hold up her skirt so high while she's doing it that people can see her underpants. Of course I don't understand why Frau Maurer was so excited about it, but I think she was right. I must write to Dolly. She's too small, she doesn't understand yet, someone must teach her to be careful.

Suddenly Renata is standing there beside my bed, and she bends and gives me a kiss. "Good night," she whispers.

I'm too shocked to answer. And then it occurs to me that today for the first time I haven't smelled my Pelikan Oil bottle. I simply forgot it.

shear the cow, milk the ram

Sundays we get to sleep longer, since we don't have breakfast until eight. I sit there and stare at my plate. Renata is sitting beside me, but I haven't said anything to her yet.

I also don't know why everything is different this morning. I woke up with an utterly dumb feeling in my stomach and I haven't dared to look at Renata. And when she asked me if we should go down to the dining room together, I didn't answer her. It is really dumb to be sitting together at the same table now too. I can't get a word out and have the feeling that everything I did last night was wrong. Renata also says nothing more, she only looks at me sideways sometimes. I hope she knows that today is another day. Yesterday is done with. Yesterday was one time. She ought to forget it.

On Sundays we have butter. I look forward to it all week long. The portion is only half as big as the portion of margarine that we get on weekdays, and even that you have to scratch on carefully if it's going to do for two slices of bread. But butter is butter. The word itself sounds pleasant. It almost rhymes with mother, of course. But it's not because of a rhyme. The word sounds pleasant because butter tastes good and because we so rarely have it. That's all.

I'm not hungry at all today, so I put all the butter on one slice of bread. If Duro got to grab my Sunday butter—that would be *lovely*.

I stare at my plate. What a crazy day. I'm all mixed up. Renata throws me a sideways glance and I act as if I don't notice it. It's painful to me. Everything is painful to me. I am a dumb cow, and something like this should never have happened to me. I've done everything wrong.

I woke up with exactly this feeling. Somehow something isn't right. Everything is wrong. "Shear the cow, milk the ram," Aunt Lou says when I act clumsy and everything I do goes awry. Aunt Lou. I have her letter in my undershirt again. How lucky that I at least didn't tell

Renata about the ten marks! I still have a few brains left; only not enough, unfortunately. I've acted like a trusting goose, like someone who doesn't know that you have to be careful. Telling stories! What a crazy idea! Oh, why did I let myself be drawn into it? I don't care what she thinks of me. And I don't want to hear her story.

Really a dumb day. After breakfast I go upstairs alone and sit at my desk. I try to write a letter to Aunt Lou. But I can't manage to do it, although only Renata is in the room. Or because she *is* in the room. However, she doesn't look at me at all anymore now, she avoids me the way I am avoiding her. Why doesn't she say anything? Really she ought to ask what's wrong with me. But I'm glad she doesn't ask, because I wouldn't know what to answer.

Why should anyone be called Renata? It's a dumb name; I don't like it at all. There was a girl in my class in my first school in Germany who was named Renata. She was mean and sneaky and always laughed the loudest when I said a word wrong. Why didn't I think of that last night?

I put my writing materials away in my schoolbag again. I don't need to hide the arithmetic notebook with the beginnings of the letter very carefully; there isn't more than the first line, "Dear Aunt Lou," in it, anyhow.

Anyone can read that. Besides, Renata wouldn't go pok-
ing around in my bookbag and take out my arithmetic
notebook and look to see what I've written in one of the
middle pages. She wouldn't do something like that, I'm
quite sure. She isn't mean or sneaky.

But it's all so painful. I told things that are nobody
else's business. I acted like an ignorant non–home kid, as
if I had no idea about real life.

I stand up, go to my wardrobe—our wardrobe—get out
my gym shorts, put them on under my skirt, and leave
the room. The entire time I haven't looked at Renata,
but I see out of the corner of my eye that she is lying on
her bed, on her side, and looking out the window at the
sky. What can she be thinking about? I would love
to know.

I go down to the ball field. Dr. Zuleger says that sports
will do me good, that they will make me a little
stronger. I can already hear Elfriede screaming, "Go on,
throw it, will you!" Yes, they are playing dodgeball. But
there are so many that a few girls are sitting on the side-
lines, in gym shorts, waiting for one of the players to
drop out. So I won't get a chance to play. I go over to the
broad-jumping pit and take off my skirt and my shoes
and socks. The black-and-blue mark on my shin has gotten pale and has a yellowish edge around it. Dumb Duro!

The sun is shining but the sand is still damp from yesterday's rain and wells up dark between my naked toes. I don't care. I take a run and jump. Again and again. This time I don't count how often I jump. I don't even put a little stick at the edge to see how far I've jumped. I simply smooth the damp sand after each jump, even though today I'm not competing against myself, and run at it again. And each time I jump I say loudly, "Damn it all!" although I don't even know what I mean by that. I don't care.

Aunt Lou. If only I had gone to see Aunt Lou yesterday. What a stupid idea that was to postpone the trip for a week. Why? In order to punish myself? It's quite all right to take for yourself what you absolutely need. I need Aunt Lou. When I don't see her for a long time I start doing dumb things. I proved that yesterday.

I jump until I have a stitch in my side and almost can't get my breath and the muscles in my legs are beginning to ache. My curses are softer now, not so angry anymore. Repeat, you have to repeat everything until it doesn't hurt. It isn't only pleasant thoughts that wear out when you think about them over and over, unpleasant ones do, too. I must remember that. Tonight I will write it in my thoughts book.

At dinner that noon, a wonderful opportunity suddenly presents itself to me. I would be dumb not to take advantage of it.

Elisabeth has table-waiting duty. She comes out of the kitchen carrying a tray with the dishes for her table. She has to pass quite close to us. At our table we have already begun to eat, because we're right next to the kitchen door. I see Elisabeth coming and quick as lightning stretch my left foot to one side. Elisabeth trips and when she crashes to the ground and all the porcelain shatters with a loud clatter, I have already pulled my foot back under the table and look just as horrified as all the others. Elisabeth begins to cry loudly, as if she were hurt. But she isn't. She stands up, stares at the floor, at the broken dishes, and weeps. For heaven's sake, it just isn't all that bad!

Many of the girls are laughing. I'm laughing too, but only inside. From the outside no one notices anything about me. I can look dumb marvelously well. I've practiced long enough. Even in front of the mirror. On the brown floor the potatoes, mixed vegetables, boiled beef, and gravy mix into an unappetizing slush. Now I see why plates are always white and never brown. The food just looks more appetizing on white.

No one noticed my foot, not even Elisabeth. She just keeps standing there dumbly, but she has stopped crying. Two girls from her table get a dustpan and brush from the kitchen and sweep up the broken dishes and the potatoes, vegetables, and meat from the floor. Fräulein Urban scolds, and Elisabeth bends, picks up the tray, and goes back to the kitchen. Fräulein Urban follows her. Now they will probably take something out of all the dishes that haven't been served yet so that Elisabeth's table will get something to eat.

I reach for my fork again. The beef now tastes particularly good to me, much better than it did before. Also the mixed vegetables, which I usually don't like very much. Duro wordlessly shoves the dish of potatoes toward me. Sundays there are a few more, so she can afford to be generous.

On the way upstairs to our room, suddenly someone behind me whispers, "You managed that beautifully."

Startled, I turn around. Rosemarie and Duro. I don't know which of the two of them said it. When people whisper, their voices are hard to recognize. "What do you mean?" I ask. But each of them makes a face as if she has no idea what I'm talking about.

Duro gives me a little push and says, "Keep moving, or are you planning to take a nap here on the stairs?"

Maybe one of them caught me putting my foot out. I don't care. Neither one of them is a tattler; they won't tell on me. And even if they do, I don't care. Then I'll do punishment duty. They can all go jump in the lake for all I care.

In the room I sit down at the desk and begin my homework. This week I've done far too little. Not only because of the collecting, but it's been an unusual week in general.

Rosemarie hasn't come back to the room. Renata is lying on her bed again, but this time she's reading. I can't tell which book. Elisabeth is sewing a dress for her dumb doll—where did she get that colorful, glittering material from?—and Dorothea is sitting with crossed legs on her bed, rummaging in her treasure box. She holds the amber bead in her hand.

She showed it to me before. It's as big as a bird's eye. And the color! Like petrified honey, with tiny bubbles and little impurities under the smooth outer surface. I would have loved to hold it for a minute that time, but Dorothea quickly put it back in her treasure box and slammed the cover and locked it. It must feel wonderful, that bead, very smooth and warm.

Dorothea notices my curious glance. She pushes the cover up so high that I can't see anymore. Dumb goose!

Nevertheless, I would love to know what she has in her treasure box.

Suddenly Elisabeth says, "Dorothea, perhaps you should keep a closer eye on your treasure box now."

Dorothea lifts her head. "Why? Everyone knows the box belongs to me. And that I would simply murder anyone who touches it."

That's true. Everyone knows about Dorothea's box, not just the girls in our room but probably everyone in the home. And even though that business about murder sounds a little bit exaggerated, I believe her capable of it. I believe Dorothea capable of a great deal.

"I'm just thinking," Elisabeth says.

I have been sitting with my back to her, but now I turn around.

She is crouching on her bed, threading a needle, and she doesn't look up as she continues to speak, but her voice sounds very hateful. "When you have the daughter of a jailbird in the room, you have to look after your things really well."

"What do you mean the daughter of a jailbird?" Dorothea asks.

I don't understand what Elisabeth means either. But then Renata begins to cry. Softly, the way she cries at night when the others are asleep. Now I look over at her.

She's turned onto her stomach, her face buried in her arms, and her back is jerking.

So that's it. But how did Elisabeth find that out? And why has she suddenly turned on Renata? The weakest. Once Elisabeth has found a victim, she doesn't let go so easily. She gibes and taunts, and you are helpless against her. The best you can do is tolerate her harassment and try not to take any notice of it, or else she carries on even worse. From the beginning, she has not been able to stand me. Of course I can't stand her, either.

Suddenly I am seized with rage. Rage at everything, at this room, at the home, and above all at Elisabeth. And also at me, because I always put up with everything from her. What does she have to be so conceited about, anyway? Just because she has parents and gets packages? Just because she is half a head taller than I am?

I spring up so recklessly that my inkwell tips over and my chair crashes against Rosemarie's bed. The ink flows over the desk and drips on the floor. But I don't care. I stand by the desk for only a moment, then I make a leap over to Elisabeth's bed, grab her by the shoulders, and shake her. "Stop it!" I scream. "Will you shut your filthy trap, for once?"

She stares at me, flabbergasted. But her astonishment doesn't last long. She lets her sewing drop, jumps off the bed, and hits me. And I—wonder of wonders—I hesitate only a moment, and then I hit back.

I have never known how very much I hate her. She hits me in the face, then I succeed in grabbing her braids and pulling on them with all my strength. She is strong, stronger than I, but I had no idea that I can also be wonderfully strong. She can't get me down. And after the first blows hit me, I feel no more pain. I stumble over her legs and fall, but I pull her with me, and we both fall to the floor. Sometimes I'm on top, sometimes she is, I don't even know whose arm is raised; I only notice when she connects with my head again. But it doesn't hurt me anymore. I kick, hit, scratch, bite. Someone is screaming very loud and piercingly. It grows dark before my eyes, but then I realize that she's the one who is screaming. She, not I! With redoubled strength I hit again. Something warm is running over my face, but I pay no attention to it. I hit. For every remark a blow, for every spitefulness a blow. For every suspicious look a blow. I scratch down her face with both hands. She's going to pay for it, she's going to pay for everything.

And then someone pulls me away from her. Fräulein Urban is standing in front of us and staring in horror and disbelief. Only now do I touch the warmth that is running down my cheeks. My fingers are red. But Elisabeth doesn't look so pretty anymore either. She stands there panting, and tears and snot run down her scratched face. There is a large spot of ink on the sleeve of her brown top. I am panting too, but I'm not crying. If Fräulein Urban weren't looking so furious, I might even be laughing. She grabs each of us by the arm and drags us along behind her to the infirmary. Elisabeth drops onto the first bed and wails. I stand at the window with my back to her and pretend that I'm looking out. Fräulein Urban goes to the telephone.

A short time later Dr. Zuleger is there. He takes care of Elisabeth first. Her right eye is swelling shut. He presses around it carefully, pulls down the lower lid, and tells Elisabeth to roll her eye. Then he mutters something inaudible and tends to the scratches on her face. He dabs them with iodine to disinfect them. I know how that burns. Elisabeth screws up her face, but she doesn't utter a sound. Then he puts bandages on the biggest scratches. "The eye will heal, but it's going to take its time," he says.

I'm next. I have a laceration on the left temple. It has begun to hurt quite a lot. "Where were you fighting, anyway?" he asks. "She couldn't have done this to you." He cleans my wound with iodine too. It burns worse than I expected. But I also don't utter a sound; I don't even screw up my face.

"Probably on the desk leg," Fräulein Urban murmurs. "They were rolling around on the floor like drunken sailors. I really don't know what to do with the two of them now."

"Oh," he says, "things like this happen sometimes, and it isn't so bad. You mustn't be too concerned about it. This young lady here will look much better in an hour when the allergic reaction has gone down. However, I must take her to the hospital; this laceration needs stitches."

I still keep gasping for air, and my head feels so empty that I'm not even really frightened.

As he packs his things into his big black bag again, he says, "You don't always have to fight it out. Come, children, make up again."

Typical grown-up. I stare at the floor.

"Come on, shake hands," he says.

I look at my hands. For the first time I see that my knuckles are bleeding. And the nail on the middle finger of my right hand is torn.

I will never shake hands with Elisabeth. Never. I put my hands behind my back. Elisabeth doesn't even move.

"Just leave them," Fräulein Urban says to Dr. Zuleger. "It will take time." Then she turns to us: "Heaven help you if something like this ever happens again! I swear to you that you can then really expect something! And what kind of a punishment you are to receive now I am going to consider very carefully."

Elisabeth looks to one side, out the window, and says not a word as Dr. Zuleger and I leave the infirmary.

better
a poor person
for a friend
than
a rich person
for an enemy

I am sitting on a chair in the treatment room. Everything smells of disinfectant and medications. I've been to hospitals before—even this one. Last year I had scarlet fever.

A nurse cuts away a little of my hair close to the wound. Then she fills a syringe. I don't show that I am afraid. I also don't show that the shot into the skin of my head hurts a damned lot; I bite my lips.

"Brave, brave," Dr. Zuleger praises. "I'm going to use four sutures. You'll feel the stitches a little."

I feel the stitches. And how. But I don't cry. Then the wound is covered with a bandage and I am finished. "I'll take you back now," says Dr. Zuleger. "And you come to me tomorrow afternoon at four and show me the wound."

I nod. The nurse presses a hard candy into my hand. "Here, you poor thing," she says, and pats my head.

"That wasn't necessary," Dr. Zuleger says, putting his arm around my shoulders. "You should have seen the other one."

We leave. In the car he asks, "Who started the fight? You or she?"

"I started fighting," I say. "But she said something mean before that."

"Ah, I see," he murmurs. Then he takes one hand from the steering wheel, pats my arm, and immediately puts his hand back. "How's your tummy doing? It's quite a long time since you've had an upset."

"That's true," I say. "I really haven't been sick for a long time. Funny, I didn't even notice."

"Be glad, then." He laughs. "Perhaps it's done you some good to have resisted for once."

Then he is silent.

Me too. I don't have any desire to talk. And besides, the stitches hurt when I move my mouth.

But when we are in front of the home and getting out, he says again, "But this fighting business is not to become a habit, you hear?"

I nod and walk toward the building.

Then we are there. I stop in front of the stairs. I don't

want to go up. I can't go up. I would prefer to just drop down there so that I needn't go up the stairs. I don't want to go up, I don't want to see anyone. Least of all Fräulein Urban or Elisabeth. My head is thundering. Perhaps I am sicker than Dr. Zuleger thinks.

He looks at me searchingly and holds out his arm. "Come, I'll help you."

If he really wanted to help me he would have kept me in the hospital. When I had scarlet fever, I liked it very well there. Susanne was there too; we caught it from one of the external students in our class.

Fräulein Urban is standing up on the landing, already waiting for us. Probably she saw us getting out of the car from her window. She has put on a fresh blouse, a white one, and she still looks very angry.

Dr. Zuleger lets go of me. "The thing is done," he says. "Halinka has behaved splendidly. I wish all my patients were as brave as she is."

He means well, but it doesn't do any good. Fräulein Urban takes me by the upper arm. "You will stay in the infirmary tonight," she says. "Your nightgown and your washing things are already there, so you needn't go into your room at all."

"Well, well," Dr. Zuleger says. "She certainly should

lie down now, but the infirmary isn't at all necessary. It's not that bad."

Fräulein Urban explains that she simply prefers to separate "the two fighting cocks" for a while. We follow her across the hallway, past the open glass door to our corridor. She opens the door to the infirmary. "Get yourself right to bed. I'll tell the infirmary duty girl that you are to get something to eat. And later I'll look in on you again."

Then she opens the door to her apartment. "Please, Doctor, come in for a moment. I would very much like to show you the new medications list."

I can't catch anything more; the door closes behind her.

The infirmary is right next to Fräulein Urban's apartment. That's a little too close for comfort, because she takes in everything—like how long you're away if you say you're only going to the toilet. Of course, when you're really sick, it has great advantages. Then she leaves both doors open at night, the one to the infirmary and the one to her apartment, and you can just call if you are feeling sick. When I had the flu, she came in the middle of the night and brought me tea. Actually she is very kind when you are sick. Really sick, I mean.

I see immediately that I am to have the bed next to

the window, because my nightie is on the blanket and *Huckleberry Finn* is on the pillow. My hand towel is hanging on the hook next to the washbasin. The bed next to the window is the nicest; I would have chosen that one too.

I undress and slip into my nightie. It's a fresh one, the blue one from my wardrobe. Suddenly I feel terribly tired, and everything hurts. I want to sleep, just sleep. Clouds waft in front of my eyes, gray and red clouds, and I feel like throwing up. The world begins to spin, slowly, then faster, the bedstead, the ceiling, the square lamps.

Then I hear the door open. I prop myself on my arms and raise my head. All at once the ceiling is overhead where it belongs, and the lamps slide back to their places.

Renata comes in. She comes straight across the room and stands beside my bed. She has her hand shoved under her sweater as if she has something hidden there.

"Thanks," she says.

She stands there a little stiffly. I can see clearly again, and I don't feel like throwing up anymore. And that dumb feeling I woke up with this morning is also gone. Perhaps I have milked the cow and shorn the ram after all?

I try to laugh, but even though the temple is a long way from the mouth, laughing hurts. "What does your mother call you, anyhow?" I ask. "Does she call you Renata?"

She blushes. "No, Rena."

We look at each other. Then suddenly she pulls out the hand under her sweater and shoves something under my covers. "I'll come back to see you after supper, if Fräulein Urban lets me," she says with an embarrassed look and quickly turns around. At the door she stops for a moment. "By the way, Dorothea and I cleaned up the ink. You almost can't see it anymore." Then she is gone.

I lift up the corner of the covers. It's a doll, a tiny, little doll, maybe four inches long. She has on a red dress, and her celluloid hair is black. But even in the dusk under the covers I can see that it's only painted black with watercolor. I lie down again and pull the covers over its head.

I've never fought with anyone before. I always thought I couldn't do it because I'm not especially big and strong. Now I'm almost a little proud. Elisabeth is older and bigger, and she wasn't able to beat me. I didn't beat her either, of course, but that's to be expected. Don't worry, Aunt Lou, I'm not planning to go out and fight everyone I can't stand, really I'm not. But I'm very glad that I can do it if necessary. You can turn sayings around, Aunt Lou. What do you think of "When a person can bite, she can feel free to show her teeth once in a while"? In any case, I'm through with taking everything from Elisabeth; that's over.

I hold the little doll in my hands and stroke her. She even has on woolen underpants. How can you knit such tiny underpants?

And then I think of a saying I want to write tonight in my thoughts book: "You should never underestimate another person, but yourself even less."

Then right away I think of something else—it'll be impossible for me to get to the luggage storeroom tonight, not from the infirmary right next to Fräulein Urban's apartment. Too bad, but there's nothing I can do about it.

I am tired; I am terribly tired.

The first blows hurt the most, Aunt Lou, because you're still so afraid. But after that it isn't so bad; it's almost as if you get used to the pain. You can just think about something else. It's only really bad at the beginning. I ought to have known that, of course; only I forgot it. Now I know it again. But when it's all over, Aunt Lou, you are tired, so tired. . . .

"Hey, wake up! You can't dream away the whole evening!"

I start up. Inge. She's standing in front of me, the tray with my food in her hands. I sit up, and she puts the tray in front of me on the bed. There's potato salad with scrambled egg.

"Duro gave you a specially big helping of scrambled egg," Inge says. "Does your head hurt?"

"Not so bad," I say. As she sets a cup of tea on the nightstand I quietly slide my little doll under the covers.

"Too bad there's a bandage over the wound," Inge says. "I'd love to see the stitches. He did give you stitches, didn't he?"

I nod. "Four."

"Did it hurt very much?"

"It could've been worse." I slide the tray with my supper to the foot of the bed and stand up. I, too, would like to see the stitches. There is a mirror over the sink by the door. It's old and has a crack on the upper left corner. Under it, on the shelf, lie my toothbrush and a broken-off piece of dentifrice stone. I stand in front of the mirror, carefully loosen the lower edge of the bandage, and lift it up. A long, red line with traces of black clotted blood and four knotted sutures. Around the wound the skin is reddish brown from the disinfectant.

Inge stands next to me. "Great!" she says admiringly. "You look really dashing. You'll probably have a scar."

"A scar on the temple isn't so bad," I say. "If I let my hair grow, people will hardly notice."

Inge looks as if she wants to say, "That'd be really stupid to cover such a lovely scar." Then she goes to the door. "I have to go back down now or Fräulein Urban will yap," she says. "See you later."

I slide the bandage into place and slip back to bed. When I reach for the fork to eat, I discover a candy under the edge of the plate. Another caramel candy from Inge. I put it on the night table for later. Duro really did dish out an especially large amount of scrambled egg, and yet I haven't much appetite. I almost have to force myself to empty the plate.

I put the tray with the plate and the fork on the desk and set my tea on the night table. Then I unwrap the caramel, stick it in my mouth, take the little doll on my lap, and open *Huckleberry Finn*.

I am just at the place where Huckleberry Finn puts the dead rattlesnake in Jim's bed when the door opens. Fräulein Urban comes in, and behind her Rena.

"Do the stitches still hurt?" asks Fräulein Urban. "Shall I give you a pain tablet?"

I shake my head. "No, that isn't necessary."

"Good," she says. "I'm going across now. If you need

something, you can knock." She pushes Rena forward. "Renata may stay with you for a while. Although you really don't deserve any kind of a privilege at all, Halinka, as you yourself know. Half an hour at most—understand, you two?"

We both nod, and she says good night and leaves.

Rena grabs a chair and sets it beside my bed. It's nicer in the luggage storeroom than here in the infirmary, although it's very bright here. But maybe that's the reason why. I hold the little doll in my hand and stroke it, and Rena talks about her mother. She really is in prison.

While Rena is talking, she plays with a narrow, light-blue ribbon that she has pulled out of her skirt pocket. I think she is ashamed and doesn't want to look at me.

"It isn't the first time," she says. "She was in prison once before, when I was seven. That time I was in a really horrible home; I just cried most of the time. This time it's even worse; this time she got two years and three months."

"What did she do?" I ask.

Rena shrugs. "I don't know exactly," she says. "The police took her, and the lady from Welfare only told me how long she's going to be away. I suppose she stole."

"What? Some money?"

"I have no idea."

"More than two years in prison just for stealing?" I don't let it show that I am frightened.

"She was in prison before," Rena says, "so they gave her more this time."

We are quiet for a while. I don't know what to say. There are some things you can't be reassuring about. Two years and three months is a long time. An eternity. But I have to say something now, something, no matter what.

At this moment Inge comes in to get the tray. "Should I bring you your breakfast tomorrow, or will you be well by then?" she asks.

"I don't know. I'm not really sick now."

She goes to the door. "Maybe you'll be lucky and won't have to go to school tomorrow. Sleep well."

We are alone again.

"And you?" asks Rena suddenly.

I stiffen. "What do you mean?"

She doesn't look at me, she just keeps pulling the light-blue ribbon between thumb and forefinger, as if she is smoothing it. Yet it's already smooth. Smooth and shining.

"Why are you here in the home?" she asks.

"My mother neglected me," I say.

Rena is quiet and wraps the light-blue ribbon around

her fingers. I am already breathing a little easier when she asks, "What does that mean, neglected? Didn't she give you anything to eat, and like that, or did she even hit you?"

"Both," I say. "My mother isn't particularly nice."

Rena stares at me in horror. "How can you say such a thing?"

"Because it's true."

"You mean, she was never good to you?" Rena asks.

I shake my head. "No."

"What about earlier," asks Rena. "When you were still little? How was she then?"

"I don't really remember then," I say. "And in between I was with Frau Kowalski. I can't remember how she was, either. I've forgotten everything. And I can't speak Polish right anymore, you know. When Aunt Lou speaks Polish, I often don't understand her. Aunt Lou says she thinks it's great that I speak German so well but that it's still too bad that I can't speak good Polish. I forget everything. I really am very forgetful, and there's nothing anyone can do about it."

"So your mother was really never good to you?" Rena asks with a trace of disbelief in her voice. Why doesn't she stop asking?

"No," I say angrily. "She really wasn't. She isn't good to anyone. I don't think she can stand anyone. Not even my aunt Lou, her very own sister. She's nasty to her, too. And now I don't want to talk about it anymore."

"Maybe she can't stand herself," Rena says. She holds up the ribbon. "Come on, I'll fix a bow in your hair."

"Blue only looks nice on blond girls," I say. "Red is better for black hair."

And suddenly there is throbbing in my temple, throbbing in my throat, throbbing behind my eyes.

Rena sits down next to me on the bed and puts my head in her lap. She strokes my hair and my face. I weep and weep.

Later, after she's gone, I think of something I must be sure to write in my thoughts book when I can get to the luggage storeroom again. "Crying is altogether different when you aren't alone. When you cry alone it's horrible."

I have a friend. She isn't strong and she isn't very useful to a person. But that doesn't matter, that means I just have to be stronger. And now I know that I can be. "Better a poor person for a friend than a rich person for an enemy," Aunt Lou would say.

I lie back, easier now. My temple is throbbing, and

my eyes are swollen. Luckily there is no one here to see me.

My little doll now has a light-blue sash over her red dress, and her black celluloid hair has light spots where my tears have fallen on it.

*a beaten dog
doesn't lick
the hand that
holds the stick*

This morning I am allowed to stay cozily in bed.

"You still look very worn out," Fräulein Urban says when she looks in on me before breakfast. "Perhaps it would be better for you not to go to school today. Just catch up on your sleep. But then you'll get up at noon, all right?"

Inge brings me breakfast. What good luck, I think, that she's the one who has infirmary duty this week and not Elfriede or Rosemarie. Rena also comes in just before school for a minute. She gives me a letter from Dolly. Susanne brought it last night.

Dolly tells in her letter about the home, about her room, about her new friend, and about Frau Maurer. All very normal. And she signs it, "Love and kisses from your friend Sigrid." So Dolly has become Sigrid. I don't need to worry about her anymore. When Susanne goes to see her sister the next time, I'll give her a real letter to take to Dolly-Sigrid.

Then I have a very pleasant morning in the infirmary with Huckleberry Finn and Miss Watson's Jim. We let ourselves float lazily down the Mississippi on our raft and talk. Huck tells about his father saying it doesn't do any harm if you borrow things, you must only intend to give them back later. But Miss Watson says that this borrowing is only another word for stealing. I think she's right, but Jim says that perhaps both are a little right, both Huck's father and Miss Watson.

It's really a lovely raft ride. During the night we see the stars in the sky, and the lights of St. Louis on the riverbank. It's quite festive. But the next day our raft is rammed by a steamboat and we are thrown into the water. I don't want to go to the Grangerfords' house with Huck because I already know what's going to happen there. So, when I surface again, I swim after Jim. We find a nice place in the reeds, let the sun dry us, and have a long discussion about blacks and slavery and things like that. Then I tell him about *Uncle Tom's Cabin*, and we both cry a little.

But now I have to get up; the gong has just rung for

dinner. At one I have to go see Fräulein Urban. I dress quickly. When I pass our room, I open the door and look in. It's empty; they're all downstairs. Only Elisabeth's stupid doll is sitting on the bed. She has on a new, color-fully glittering dress. I glance at her without interest. I have a doll of my own, one with black hair, even if the color is a little bit smeary. There is no one left in the corridor or on the stairs. I am very late and the last one to enter the dining room.

The others lift their heads and stare at me as I go to my table. Rena smiles at me, and Inge takes a plate full of soup from her tray and puts it at my place. "I was just about to bring you your food," she says. "Now at least I don't have to balance sloshing lentil soup all the way up the stairs."

Duro looks up from her plate and touches her hand to her left temple. "Does it hurt very much?" she asks.

I shake my head. "No, no. It really isn't so bad."

Carefully I cast a glance over toward Elisabeth's table. She has only two bandages on her face still, one on the left cheek and one on her forehead, but you can't miss her black eye, even at this distance.

"Four stitches!" Inge says this so proudly that it sounds as though she put them in herself.

"And the doctor said she never let out a peep while he was doing it," Rena adds.

How does she know that? Before I can ask, she continues, "Fräulein Urban told us that herself when she told us about it."

Obviously the fight has been discussed throughout the home. They keep looking over at me from the other tables. I don't know exactly what the looks mean. I almost have the feeling that I'm the heroine of the day. But I'm not entirely certain. Luckily Rena is sitting next to me. What a wonderful coincidence that we sit at the same table.

"Anyhow, it's a good thing you finally showed her," Duro says. "Now she'll leave you alone." She fishes a little piece of bacon out of the soup. "What was it all about, anyhow? Why did you fight?"

That obviously has not been discussed yet; the others must have kept quiet about that. I look sideways over at Rena. She is sitting upright and clearing her throat as if she wants to say something, but at first she can't get any words out. She coughs, and then she says it after all.

"My mother's in prison," she says. "That's why I'm here. Elisabeth was trying to upset me about it, and Halinka stood up for me. That's why they fought."

I lower my head over my plate and don't dare to look up. Why did she say that? You just don't do that. Now everyone at the table knows her mother is in prison, and by early tomorrow morning, at the latest, everyone in the home will know it. Bad words have wings, and once you've spoken them, you can never take them back, even if you'd like to.

Inge lets out an admiring whistle. Why? Is your mother being in prison something?

"Fantastic," Inge says. "I think it's fantastic that you told. Now you don't need to be afraid that the others will find out."

Rena doesn't say anything, she only blushes a little and drops her head. I don't say anything either. What a strange idea! To humiliate yourself so that you don't have to be afraid of humiliation anymore? I must really think about Inge again. Later sometime, for now I can only think about Fräulein Urban. The last time I had to go see her it was not particularly pleasant. Quite the contrary.

"What's it like, exactly, when you have to go see Fräulein Urban?" Rena asks as we climb the stairs. "What does she do?"

I shrug with more indifference than I'm feeling. "First she gives a sermon, and then she pronounces your punishment. Nothing special. Don't worry. She never hits, not even if you've been ordered to come see her."

The last time it was the business of the fifty-pfennig piece, and Fräulein Urban was quite angry then. No going out for four Sundays and two weeks of kitchen duty. Naturally Elisabeth didn't get any punishment; she was just the poor victim who I had stolen from. And of course it didn't occur to Fräulein Urban to ask her what she'd had in mind when she filed the notch in the edge of the coin.

I go quickly to the washroom, wet my face, and run my damp hands through my hair. Rena stands beside me, watching. "I'll keep my fingers crossed for you," she says.

She means well, but it probably won't do any good. I get my little doll from her place in my wardrobe and slide her into my skirt pocket. Good that my skirt pocket is big and the doll is so small. Then it's two minutes to one and I go.

When I knock on Fräulein Urban's door, she immediately says, "Come in."

She's sitting in her living room on the sofa and waves me to the armchair on her left, beside the closed door to her bedroom. No one has ever seen that; the door is always closed.

Elisabeth is sitting in the armchair on the right. The scratch on her nose stands out, and her eye is a mixture of purple, crimson, and violet. Orchid colors. In the big chair she looks smaller than usual, more humble somehow.

"Well," says Fräulein Urban, when I have sat down. "Do you want to talk about why you fought?"

I shake my head; Elisabeth too.

"I thought not. Now, you probably had a reason, but we'll pass over that. I'll start from the fact that you both are equally to blame in this unhappy affair. Is there any possibility that you will reconcile with each other?"

Again I shake my head. What an idea, to reconcile with Elisabeth. A beaten dog doesn't lick the hand that holds the stick. I will write that in my thoughts book when I have the chance. And perhaps also the saying "Blows don't bring love." That's certainly true too.

It almost makes me laugh. So I stare rigidly at the radio that is sitting on the table next to the sofa. A big brown box. On the front, over the long strip with the many city names and the buttons on each side, there is a round hole and stretched tight behind it is a light-brown material with dark-brown dots in it. Aunt Lou has almost the exact same radio.

Fräulein Urban talks and talks. "When so many people

have to live together the way they do here in the home, they have to find a way to get along with one another. And when you get older you can't simply lash out when you don't like something." And so on and so on.

When I go to see Aunt Lou on Saturday she'll be shocked and ask why I have the bandage on my temple. What shall I say then? Perhaps I should go a week later, when I won't have a bandage any longer? But that won't help, either. I'll still have a scar, Dr. Zuleger said. "But it's not so bad on the temple. When your hair grows a little longer, it will hardly show." But hair doesn't grow so fast, especially not the strip that the nurse cut off before the stitches. Aunt Lou will see it in any case. Of course, I can simply say I fell. I'll see.

"You will have to live together until the end of the school year," Fräulein Urban is saying. "When the rooms are changed, I will separate you. Can you both manage until then without knocking each other on the head?"

"If that one there will keep her claws in," Elisabeth murmurs and carefully runs her fingertip from her black eye to the scratch on her nose.

Fräulein Urban laughs, but it isn't a joyful laugh. "Stop playing the little innocent here, Elisabeth. I know my girls. So, how's it to be? I require a definite answer."

"If she quits making those remarks," I say and secretly

put my hand in my skirt pocket where the little doll is hiding.

"Good." Fräulein Urban nods. "Each of you leave the other one alone. You don't have to be friends, but one *can* require you to leave each other alone. Promise me that nothing like this will occur again?"

Elisabeth nods without looking up. I nod too.

"And furthermore," Fräulein Urban continues, "you will receive the following punishments: you, Elisabeth, will do two weeks of dishwashing duty, starting tomorrow. And you, Halinka, two weeks of kitchen duty. I will advise Frau Breitkopf and Frau Koch today. Do you agree to your punishments?"

Both of us reply, "Yes."

Fräulein Urban always asks if we agree to our punishments. As if we have a choice. Anyway, I've never heard that she's ever wavered in imposing her penalties. Somebody ought to try it sometime.

Then we are dismissed. I am just going to open the door to the infirmary when Fräulein Urban calls after me, "You're back in your room from now on, Halinka. That's the end of being sick."

I straighten the bed covers and gather my things together. There isn't much. *Huckleberry Finn,* toothbrush, nightie, and hand towel. Then I go to our room. I push down the door handle with my elbow.

Elisabeth isn't in the room, I see at once. Dorothea is lying on her bed. "Well?" she asks curiously. "What kind of a punishment did you get?"

I don't answer, just shrug.

Rena is sitting at the desk, doing homework. Now she stands up and takes me by the hand. "Come on," she says.

We sit on the stairs to the dining room and I tell her what happened with Fräulein Urban. When I tell her the punishment, she begins to laugh.

"What's so funny about that?" I ask angrily. "Two weeks of kitchen duty. Two weeks, Monday to Friday, sitting in the kitchen for two long hours peeling potatoes. It doesn't sound very funny to *me*."

She puts her arms around my neck and gives me a kiss. On the stairs, where everyone can see us. A strange girl. She just kisses when she feels like it. I will have to get used to that. I can hardly say to her that it's uncomfortable for me, that would be even more uncomfortable.

"No, but it's much, much better than dishwashing duty," Rena says. "A suitable punishment for you. Fräulein Urban always finds just the right thing. I realized

that recently when she gave Susanne two weeks of reception duty—remember?"

Of course I remember; it was only a few weeks ago.
Susanne just disappeared from the home one afternoon.
I have no idea how she did it or what she told Herr
Breitkopf, but in any case, she was gone. It came out
because she tried to steal a few tulips and got caught.
Well, that can happen. Really, stealing tulips isn't so bad,
so long as you don't get caught; but Susanne didn't have
permission to go out that day, and that was bad. Her
punishment was to sit from two to seven in the reception room for two weeks.

Whoever has reception duty has to take phone calls
and get the person who's being called. Although we don't
get many calls, you also have to enter on a list the names
of all the girls who go out, and of course you also have to
note when they come back. And on days when no one is
supposed to go out you have to check to be sure they
have a pass from Fräulein Urban. It's a dumb job. You
don't really have to work the way you do when you have
dishwashing or kitchen duty, so reception lasts for five
hours. You're also supposed to do your homework during
this period, because we have supper at seven, and afterwards there isn't enough time. Five hours is a long time,

and you really can't do anything. It isn't even possible to read because you only have about fifteen minutes uninterrupted at the most. A day of reception duty is a wasted day.

"That was good of Fräulein Urban to give Susanne reception as a punishment," Rena says. "And it's also good that she sentenced you to kitchen duty. You always get something extra to eat there, everyone says, and you really are very thin. Now you'll get fed every day for two weeks. That's for sure."

She's right. The good thing about kitchen duty is the extra food. Frau Koch is so fat that she thinks every girl in the home is undernourished. But kitchen duty really does mean peeling potatoes the whole time. Potatoes for the entire home. I don't like that work.

Suddenly I remember something. I run up the few steps and look at the big clock. Three-thirty.

"What's the matter?" Rena asks.

"I have to be at Dr. Zuleger's at four."

"I'll go with you," she offers.

To my surprise, Fräulein Urban gives us permission. "Then at least Halinka won't get into any trouble on the way," she says as she signs the passes. "And, Halinka, put on another blouse. That one has ink spots from yesterday."

It's true. So I put on the old blue one, the one from the home, and over it my green windbreaker. Then we take off. An unexpected outing! And with a friend. When we are far enough away from the home so that no one can see us anymore, we hold hands.

what

does the chicken

dream of?

millet,

nothing but

millet

*E*veryone is there, all fifteen girls who collected for the Mothers' Convalescent League. The sixteenth is Susanne, who came with her friend Claudia and the new girl in the fifth grade. "Frau Lehmann is coming at seven-forty-five," Fräulein Urban announced at supper. "Please be punctual."

We are punctual, of course. Everyone is talking at once, and Susanne, who is sitting next to me, is betting with the new girl for a round of dishwashing duty about who will win the prize. The new one points to Claudia, and Susanne bets on me. If she only knew! Suddenly I'm afraid again that maybe they saw that I'd broken into the box. What shall I say then? Here, in front of all the others! Perhaps I'd better go away and hide.

I'm still mulling this over when Fräulein Urban comes in. Beside her is the local representative. A few girls begin to giggle. It's the lilac-gray oh-god-oh-god, Fräulein Urban's bosom friend. We didn't know that her name is Lehmann and that she's the local representative for the Mothers' Convalescent League. Susanne kicks my leg under the table. But only gently. I turn my head to her. She winks at me, I wink back.

The lilac-gray oh-god-oh-god has a black briefcase, which she now places in front of her on the cutting table.

"Now, dear children," she begins to sing, "I would like to thank you all in the name of the Mothers' Convalescent League for collecting so diligently."

"The prize," the new one calls out. "Who gets the prize?"

"Oh-god-oh-god, I almost forgot that," trills the local representative. The giggles get louder. Fräulein Urban frowns, and everyone becomes quiet.

The lilac-gray oh-god-oh-god pulls a folded piece of paper from the pocket of her lilac-colored skirt and opens it. "Now, the champion collector at seventy-one marks sixty-seven is your friend Halinka. Halinka, stand up."

There are disappointed sighs. Susanne claps loudly and a few others join in.

This can't be true, I simply can't believe it. The ten marks are still lying, carefully wrapped in newspaper, behind my beam. Or did I only dream that? No, you can't dream something so complicated. And certainly not this fear about the wire and the stupid seal.

Susanne again kicks my leg, this time harder. "Didn't you hear?" she hisses. "You're supposed to stand up."

Then the local representative is already standing in front of me and holding out her hand. I leap up.

"Hearty congratulations," she says, smiling, and she shakes my hand. Her hand is very soft and she shakes very gently. She's been eating garlic; I can smell it clearly. All at once she seems much less strange to me. Aunt Lou likes garlic too.

"And what is it, the prize?" Claudia asks.

Two tables over, Elisabeth gets up. You can tell from looking at her how angry she is; she doesn't even make any effort to be quiet. Without saying a word she walks past the local representative and leaves the handicrafts room. She slams the door behind her. The local representative stares after her in shock.

"She's really mad, the silly goose," Susanne whispers rather loudly.

The local representative keeps looking over at the door and is about to say something, but Fräulein Urban has walked over to her and lays a hand on her arm. The local representative says nothing.

"The prize," says Fräulein Urban loudly, "is an utterly marvelous excursion to Schwetzingen Castle Park, in the car. The outing also includes ice cream and a meal in a restaurant."

No bicycle. Of course not, I knew that. But it could at least have been a book. Or a paint box with twenty-four colors.

"On this coming Wednesday, in fact, if the weather is nice enough," continues Fräulein Urban, looking at me. "If not, the outing will be postponed for a week. It has to be a Wednesday because that's the only day that Herr Lehmann doesn't need the car himself."

Not that I have anything against outings! I love to go on outings with Aunt Lou. Then we pack something to eat, take some streetcar line or other to the last stop, and wander around the countryside. We climb up mountains and clamber around in castle ruins. But drive with the local representative of the Mothers' Convalescent League to Schwetzingen Castle Park? What's so great about that! Why doesn't she go there alone, if she wants to go there so badly, and give me the money she would have spent for the meal and the ice cream? What do I care about Schwetzingen Castle Park? I would so much rather have had a book—for instance, a *Huckleberry Finn* for my very own. I know I can think of lots of other things that I would love to have. Anyway, something you can hold in your hand. Aunt Lou would say, "What does the chicken dream of? Millet, nothing but millet." My millet just doesn't happen to be the Schwetzingen Castle Park.

Meanwhile the local representative has gone back to the cutting table, opened her black briefcase, and taken out a very large brown paper bag. "And now, there is candy for everyone who collected," she says. "Please come up to the table."

"Get in line!" calls Fräulein Urban, but no one is paying any attention to her anymore. Everyone crowds around the local representative, who disappears in the swarm of girls. I'm the only one still sitting down.

Susanne grins at me when she comes back sucking on a candy. The local representative hasn't noticed at all that Susanne didn't collect. Apparently Fräulein Urban hasn't either. Or she doesn't want to say anything. "Great," mutters Susanne, shoving the candy into the corner of her right cheek so that she looks as if she had mumps. "You brought me luck. Elke has to do dishwashing duty for me when it's my turn again." So the new fifth-grader is named Elke.

Then the local representative comes up to me and presses five candies into my hand. Lemon drops, wrapped in yellow paper. I shove them into my skirt pocket.

The others are all talking at once until Fräulein Urban claps her hands loudly a few times. "So. Now go to your rooms and start getting ready for bed. And, of course, don't forget to wash, either. After all, I know my girls."

I am about to stand up too, but she holds me back. I let myself fall into the chair, and Fräulein Urban and the local representative also sit down.

Fräulein Urban's voice sounds excited when she begins to talk. We'll leave on Wednesday, right after fourth period, because I don't take religious instruction. She's also coming with us—Herr Sauer has agreed to substitute for her. "I'm so looking forward to the trip," she says.

I look at her. For the first time it occurs to me that she's always in the home too. She came long before me and will still be here after I—I hope, I hope—am long gone. She will never get out, never. Every year children leave, and every year new ones come, and she is always still here. She will get older and older and older, and finally she will die here, in her bedroom, without ever . . .

"Did you ever actually see an orchid, Fräulein Urban?" I ask.

She looks at me in astonishment. Then she shakes her head. "No, not yet. I only know them from books. What made you think of that?"

"Oh, I just did," I say. "I haven't ever seen one either. But I would like to."

"I saw an orchid once," says the local representative. "Beautiful white orchids with red and yellow spots way down in the throat, and with large, strangely shaped, irregular petals. They looked magnificent, really bizarre."

"I thought orchids were violet, purple, and crimson," I say in disappointment. "And what does *bizarre* mean?"

"It means fantastic, peculiar," says Fräulein Urban.

"There are also violet orchids, of course," the local representative says. It sounds almost apologetic. She can't help it that she saw white orchids. But she seems to be sorry about it. "I know that there are also violet orchids," she continues, "but I personally have only seen white ones."

She looks at me inquiringly and concerned. Attentively, somehow, as if she wants to be sure to find out what I want to hear.

Fräulein Urban puts her arm around my shoulders. "What's the matter, Halinka?"

I quickly free myself. "Nothing," I say. "I was only imagining something." I turn sideways, to the local representative. "How big were the flowers of the orchids that you saw?"

With hands cupped she describes something the size of a doll's head. Of course, I mean the head of Elisabeth's doll, not mine.

"And what were they like?" I ask again. "Were they glistening or glowing or soft, almost dull?"

The local representative thinks some more. "I think they were rather soft," she says. "Is that the way you imagined them?"

I nod. It's no good. She really wants to do me a favor, even if I don't understand why. But it doesn't help. I think I will have to wait until I see an orchid myself someday. I'm not one of those people who believes everything people tell them. I believe you more than anyone, Aunt Lou. But in this case I wouldn't even believe you, for you would have known ahead of time how I imagine orchids, and you would have described them exactly that way because you wouldn't want to disappoint me. I'm not angry with you about that. But, all the same. A half-truth is a whole lie, Aunt Lou; you say that yourself all the time.

I feel strangely depressed and sad. I would rather be in bed and stroking my little doll under the covers.

I stand up. "I'm tired, I have to go to bed."

"Are you in pain?" Fräulein Urban asks.

I nod. She offers me a pain tablet again, but I decline it. Something is hurting me, but it isn't the wound in my temple. A half-truth is a whole lie. And besides, I don't want them to notice how disappointed I am. I don't want to spoil the fun for them. The local representative is nice, and Fräulein Urban seems to be looking forward to the outing very much.

"Well, then, until Wednesday," says the local representative, holding out her hand to me. "Let's hope the weather cooperates."

"Yes, let's hope," I say, giving her my hand and quickly pulling it back again.

Later, when the others are finally asleep, Rena and I slip away to the luggage storeroom.

"Well?" she asks, when we are sitting on the koldra. "Are you excited about the excursion?"

"I would rather have had a book," I say. "Oh well, I can't do anything about it. The lilac-gray oh-god-oh-god is a strange woman. I think she really does think that's a wonderful prize. But what do I need with stupid old Schwetzingen Castle Park?"

Rena looks at me thoughtfully. "I don't understand you. I would be looking forward to it."

"Do you want my prize? Shall I give it to you?"

She shakes her head. "No, it belongs to you. But enjoy it. An outing is always better than the home, isn't it? And besides, you'll get ice cream."

Suddenly I feel better. She's right. An excursion with ice cream and going to a restaurant, even with Fräulein Urban and Frau Lehmann, is nothing to sneeze at. And my real prize, the only one that's important to me, I have already.

Suddenly Rena looks very strange, the candle throwing trembly shadows over her face. She looks at me almost fearfully, as if she is waiting for me to help her. The way Dolly looked when Frau Maurer was so angry at her.

"What's the matter?" I ask. "Has something bad happened?"

Rena drops her head. "I have to tell you my story," she says. "One I'm ashamed of."

"That's a dumb game," I say. "We should never have started it. Whose idea was it, anyhow, yours or your friend's?"

She lifts her head, and now her face is normal again. "Hers. But I still have to tell you the story, this once. One story for the other, shame for shame. After that we can both be certain that neither of us can do anything to the other."

As far as I'm concerned, it isn't necessary, but if she really wants to . . . "All right," I say, "but this is the last story, and then we're not doing it anymore."

She nods. And then she begins to tell.

She was playing on the street, hide-and-seek with her friend and other children in the neighborhood. She saw the police car stop in front of her building and was immediately afraid. It wasn't the first time, although she couldn't really remember the time before very well, when she was in second grade. She stood there frozen as two policemen got out of the car and went into the building. She stood beside the car, right next to it, and she couldn't move a muscle. When the policemen came back out of the building, they had Rena's mother between them and led her to the car. Her mother looked at Rena, but Rena turned her head away. She didn't go up to her and say good-bye; she turned around and ran away. Later, a lady from Welfare came and brought her to the home.

"I was ashamed," Rena says. "I ran away so that the policemen wouldn't see that I'm her daughter. Now I'm so sorry. I should have stuck by her. I should have told her that I love her. When I think about it, it makes me cry."

I don't know what to say. I understand, and I also don't

understand. If my mother were taken away by the police, I'd probably be glad, not ashamed. Perhaps I should imagine how I would feel if Aunt Lou were taken away by the police. But something like that would never happen. Anyway, that's what I think. But you never know, of course.

Rena is crying. I would like to take her head on my lap, the way she did with me, but I can't do that. I can't even just give someone a kiss the way she does. Even thinking about it I freeze. I stroke my little doll.

"Have you seen your mother since then?" I ask.

She shakes her head. "No."

"Have you written to her?"

Again she shakes her head. "I don't know what to write to her. I'm so ashamed."

"If your mother really loves you," I say, and I think of Aunt Lou, "then you can just explain it to her and she'll understand."

Rena wipes away her tears. "Do you honestly think so?"

"Yes," I say firmly. "I think so."

In reality, I'm not so certain, but I can't say that to Rena. She looks reassured. Sometimes it isn't the best thing to tell the truth.

Because neither of us can think what to say, I stand up,

get my thoughts book out of its hiding place, and open it. There is still a stump of a pencil at the last entry.

I hold the book out to Rena. "Here. Do you want to write something in it?"

Rena lays it on her knee. She stares at the paper for a long time without moving. "I can't think of a saying," she says finally.

I sit down beside her and take the book out of her hand. At first I can't think of a saying either, but then I write slowly and carefully: "A half-truth is a whole lie. But perhaps that's not so. Perhaps a half-truth is just a half-truth."

Now Rena laughs, and the candlelight is no longer mysterious but makes her face pretty and almost joyful. She takes the book out of my hand and writes: "And when you have a friend, half- or whole truths don't matter anymore."

*while one
holds the cow
by the horns,
the other
can milk her*

Frau Koch is sitting at the big kitchen table. In front of her is a board and a heap of dry bread. She's cutting it into small pieces with a knife and then tipping them into a pan. Cut-up bread means that we'll be getting bread fritters either for supper or tomorrow noon. I really love bread fritters, especially when Frau Koch sprinkles a little extra sugar on them.

When we come in, she raises her head and surveys us with surprise. "How come there are two of you?" she asks. "Fräulein Urban only mentioned Halinka."

"She said we could," Rena says quickly. "And she said we only need to work for one hour because there are two of us."

"Is that so?" Frau Koch asks suspiciously.

"Honestly. You can even ask her."

Of course Frau Koch will never climb up to the third floor just for that, which Rena knows perfectly well. But Fräulein Urban really did say we could; I was amazed too. Rena said to her that since she was the cause of the fight, it would be only right that she should also share in the punishment.

"But you probably don't want to help Elisabeth with dishwashing duty, or do you?" Fräulein Urban asked with a laugh.

Frau Koch grumbles that no one ever tells her anything right, that she is only the servant for everyone else, that no one ever discusses anything with her, and no one takes her seriously. She grumbles more and more softly, until finally we can't understand her anymore.

What's she getting so excited about? She's getting the same help, after all. Two times one hour instead of one times two hours. It has to be the same to her.

We stand there and wait until she finally calms down. Then she points to two big buckets of washed potatoes that are waiting for us.

"There's potato soup tonight," she says. "Get to work." She looks at Rena. "What's your name, anyhow? You've never been here before."

"Renata," Rena says. "I haven't been in the home very long."

So there won't be bread fritters until tomorrow. Too bad. Rena picks up a bowl for the peels and a small paring knife, sits down on a stool in front of one of the potato buckets, and falls to work. First I get a large pot for the peeled potatoes and fill it with water, because potatoes turn brown and ugly in the air. These aren't exactly nice looking anyway; they're from last fall and already have blackish places and many small eyes that you can't quite get all out. New potatoes don't come in until September or October. The old ones are soft and wrinkled and have long, white shoots, which you have to cut off, and they are very hard to peel. With new potatoes, on the other hand, it's almost fun.

I also take a bowl and a knife and sit down opposite Rena.

Frau Koch has finally regained her calm. "Why did you get kitchen duty, anyway, Halinka?" she asks curiously. "Does it have something to do with your bandage? What happened?"

"Nothing," I say quickly. "I just fell."

If only the things weren't so soft. I cannot stand potato peeling. Frau Koch can't either, I guess—I never do anything else on kitchen duty except peel potatoes.

"How often do people have kitchen duty?" asks Rena, who obviously has thoughts similar to mine.

Frau Koch laughs. "There's someone here almost every day, sometimes even two or three. You aren't particularly good girls, so things happen pretty easily, and all at once someone is sitting there."

Not good girls! What does Frau Koch know about anything? She never comes up into the home. "That must be all right with you," I say. "That way you never have to peel potatoes yourself."

Now she's angry again, although I didn't mean it to be nasty. Well, maybe a little bit. "You probably think you do the work and I get paid for it," she scolds. "I know what you think about me: the dumb, fat old thing in the kitchen. Yes, you think that, I know well enough."

Of course it's true, but naturally I don't say so. And not just because Rena nudges me so hard that I almost cut my finger. No, I don't want to get on the wrong side of Frau Koch; that wouldn't pay. Especially not when my punishment duty is just beginning.

"No," Rena says, "we really don't think that. You are very good to us, Frau Koch. Everyone says so."

Frau Koch mutters for a little while longer, then she stops cutting bread. "Show me what you have under that bandage," she says.

I willingly stand up, go over to her, and bend down. The bandage is easy to loosen because I've been checking myself to see how the wound looks. The stitches are coming out on Friday.

Frau Koch stares at my stitches for a long time. "Poor child," she says and puts down her knife. "I think I'll just make you some hot milk." She goes to the stove. "Or don't you want some hot milk?"

Is there anyone who doesn't like hot milk? "Yes," we say in unison, "we'd love it."

While the milk is heating, Frau Koch roots around in a large, black shopping bag that is standing in the corner next to the kitchen cupboard. "I bought bananas today," she says. "For myself personally, for supper. I'll share them with you. We'll have a delicious little snack for ourselves."

She pulls out five bananas and lays them on the table. Did she really intend to eat them all by herself? No wonder she is so fat. My mouth is watering. I have only had bananas a few times in my life, but I remember exactly how they taste.

Rena flashes a grin at me. "Didn't I tell you?" she whispers.

It's much easier to get along with Frau Koch when there are two of us than when I am alone with her. Once again I think of one of Aunt Lou's sayings: "While one holds the cow by the horns, the other can milk her." Not that I think of Frau Koch as a cow; it's just a saying.

Frau Koch spreads a few slices of bread. With butter, not with margarine—I'm watching. Of course, she doesn't spread the butter as thick as your finger, like in the sanatorium that time, but she doesn't scratch it across the bread, either. Then she takes the pan from the stove and pours the milk into three cups.

"So, come on, my ducks."

The two ducks swiftly drop their knives and flutter to the table. You almost always get a slice of bread when you have kitchen duty, but rarely hot milk. And I have never, ever heard anything about bananas.

It really is a delicious little snack. I eat the bread from the edge in—first the crust, then all around. Then, with my teeth, I push the butter to the middle. In the end there is a tiny bit of bread with a whole mountain of butter left, which I then put in my mouth all at once. But I don't chew it, I press it against my palate slowly with my tongue until the butter has spread all through my mouth. What a beautiful feeling! At Aunt Lou's I always eat bread and butter that way. Not here in the home, of course; it won't work with scratched-on butter.

While we are chewing ecstatically, Frau Koch remarks,

"We have to be grateful to the Americans for the bananas. They brought them from America. Before the war, I never saw a banana."

"In America they have everything," Rena says. "Bananas and oranges and cocoa and everything. And in New York there are skyscrapers. Those are buildings with fifty or a hundred floors."

Frau Koch nods. We have each eaten a banana, and there are still two left. She reaches for one of them. And then her good heart triumphs and she pushes both bananas over to us. "Here, eat them," she says. "You both need them more than I do."

I peel my second banana. The peel is yellow, with brown speckles at the ends. The fruit is almost white and fragrant. It is a special aroma, unlike any other. Really, only bananas smell that way. I inhale deeply once more. Maybe I can manage to make a mental note of the smell. Maybe I can smell it again in bed tonight.

"In New York there are no sunsets," I say.

"Why not?" Frau Koch asks in astonishment.

"Because you can't see the horizon. There are way too many buildings, and they're so tall that you can't see the horizon. It has to be a really huge sunset there for people to be able to see it."

"All the things you know!" Frau Koch says.

"How *do* you know, anyway?" Rena asks. "You were never in New York. Did you read it? Is that in *Huckleberry Finn*?"

I shake my head. "No, of course not. Huckleberry Finn lived on a river, on the Mississippi. And I was only in Poland. But my aunt Lou knows it, and she told me."

"Has your aunt Lou ever been to America?" Frau Koch asks with her mouth full.

"No." I take the second slice of bread and butter that she is holding out to me and bite into the banana once again, then into the bread. "No, she hasn't been there. But she says that a person can imagine. She says that you can imagine almost everything, if you only think about it right."

The banana tastes fantastic; the bread and butter, too. I am now chewing very slowly, in order to keep some of it for as long as possible, and I resolve never to say bad things about kitchen duty again. And especially not about Frau Koch.

Suddenly Rena asks, "And how are the sunsets in Poland?"

I have to think about that for a while. I don't know anymore; I can't remember a single sunset in Poland. I remember almost nothing about Poland.

"Normal," I say. "So-so. Not particularly beautiful,

not particularly bad. In Poland everything is so-so, I guess."

We are quiet for a while. Then Frau Koch says, "Where I come from, there are marvelous sunsets. The whole sky gets red, as if the world is on fire. Until the sun goes down behind the sea."

"Did you live by the sea?" asks Rena.

And I ask, "Are there palm trees and white sand there?"

She laughs loudly. "Where did you get an idea like that? No, there are no palm trees in East Prussia. Some white sand, though, but only in summer. In winter it rains a lot and the sand gets grayish-brown. Then it looks gray and rippled, like a washboard, from the tides and the waves." Suddenly she looks very sad. "And instead of palms we have birches. And beach grass and broom."

She sets her partly eaten bread back on the table.

"Is it that beautiful where you lived?" Rena asks. "Do you ever get homesick?"

"What do you know about that?" she says. "You're much too young for that. What do you know about homesickness yet?" She turns to Rena. "What do you call home?"

"Where my mother is," Rena says.

"And for you?" Now she's looking at me.

"I have no home," I say. That's all I can get out. Although it's only a half-truth. Because I really ought to say "Where my aunt Lou is." But then Frau Koch will ask me why my aunt, and don't I have a mother. "I was born in Poland," I say quickly, "but I don't think of Poland as my home."

The mood in the kitchen is different all of a sudden. Sad and depressed. I feel tears welling in my eyes. Frau Koch also looks as though she's about to cry. She passes the back of her hand across her eyes, first the right one over the right eye, then the left one over the left.

Suddenly she gives herself a shake. "Foolishness," she says loudly. "All foolishness. Home, that's a few pictures you keep in your head. No, I'm not homesick, although I would dearly love to see the sea again. If I could, I would live by the sea. But if it doesn't happen, then it doesn't happen. If you mean by homesickness, Renata, that I yearn to go back to earlier days, then I can only say no. I didn't have the kind of home that makes me yearn to go back to it. My father was strict, my mother even stricter. We had nothing to laugh about. Nothing to laugh about and nothing to eat. No, I don't have any homesickness.

Only a few pictures in my head. The sunsets, for instance. Birches under a gray sky. And the sea and the dunes."

"What are dunes?" Rena asks.

Frau Koch shakes her head. "Sometimes you are so smart, and sometimes you know very little at all. Dunes are sand piles, hills, that build up along the shore. Like waves of sand from the waves of water."

She stands up, puts the empty cups in the sink, and reaches for her knife. The strange mood passes, and all at once kitchen duty is exactly the same as it always is. Peeling potatoes. But I still have the taste of bananas in my mouth.

I try very hard to work well and to peel the potatoes as thin as Frau Koch wants them, although that is anything but easy with potatoes that are so old and soft already. When we are done, she praises us and pats our heads.

"I'll think up another nice snack for tomorrow," she promises.

"We aren't coming tomorrow," I say. "If the weather is good, I skip kitchen duty tomorrow because I'm going away. But then starting the day after tomorrow we'll be here every day."

As we climb the stairs, Rena says, "Funny. I guess everyone has memories they don't like to think about. I guess everyone has something they're ashamed of and don't want to talk about."

I just nod. I'm not surprised. I've always known it. And even Aunt Lou gets sad and avoids some questions. So I never ask about what happened earlier.

In the room the others are busy tidying up their wardrobes. Pieces of clothing are lying on beds and chairs.

"What's going on?" I ask.

Susanne thumps her winter boots on the floor. "Wardrobe inspection," she says angrily. "Elfriede just ran through the corridor with the gong. Fräulein Urban is doing a wardrobe inspection this evening. Someone must have made her very angry, and now we have to pay for it. Get going, clean up. I have no desire to get demerits for the room just because of you."

Elisabeth is carefully folding her doll's clothes. She doesn't look up when we come in. We haven't yet spoken one word to each other, she and I. That's nothing unusual; we didn't before, either. But now she also seems not to be speaking with the others. Why, I wonder. Is she angry or is she embarrassed?

Dorothea wipes off her treasure box with a damp washcloth before she puts it back in the wardrobe.

Rosemarie hangs her beautiful blue dress with the

embroidered collar and the wide, flaring skirt neatly on a hanger. She has the most work; her wardrobe always looks as if rabbits have been burrowing in it. First she shared a wardrobe with Elisabeth, but when one became empty because Doris went back to her parents, Elisabeth insisted that Rosemarie get the single wardrobe in the room. You couldn't expect anyone to share the wardrobe with her, she said, and that was true. Rosemarie is a slob.

Not Rena. Her things lie exquisitely folded in the wardrobe. "Come on," she says, "I'll help you. Let's start right now."

So we do. I quickly take the little doll out of her hiding place in my underthings and slide her under my pillow, where she always is when I am in the room. Then I take the things out of the cupboard, and Rena and I fold them up neatly before we put them back again. Rena lifts my red blouse. "I'll wash it for you later," she says, "so you can wear it for your outing tomorrow."

I look at her in amazement. Naturally I am very happy that she is going to wash my blouse for me, but it's a little funny, nevertheless.

"Don't worry," she says. "I know how to do it. I often did the washing for us at home."

While we tidy up the wardrobe, I am thinking the

entire time about Frau Koch and the excursion to Schwetzingen, about Poland, about the sea, which I've never seen, and about the park that I will see tomorrow. If the weather is good.

And I still have the taste of bananas in my mouth.

*god
takes his time,
but
he repays
with interest*

The weather is not only good, it's downright marvelous. The sun is radiant, and the air feels as if it were already midsummer.

We are sitting in the car. In front are Frau Lehmann, the local representative of the Mothers' Convalescent League, dressed entirely in lilac, as usual, and next to her Fräulein Urban. She is wearing a light-blue blouse and a dark-blue pleated skirt. In back are Wolfi, Frau Lehmann's son, and I. I only learned that he was coming while I was waiting for the car with Fräulein Urban. "Wolfi is coming too," she said, "so you won't be all by yourself." Wolfi! What a name! I almost asked if he was out of diapers yet.

He looks to be ten at the most, but he is eleven, he says. If only he would keep his mouth shut. But he keeps having to say something. "The car is brand-new," he says proudly. I nod. Fräulein Urban has already told me. It is beige and shiny.

Wolfi asks what my name is, what grade I am in, if I have a friend, if it's nice in the home, how I managed to collect so much money. I answer reluctantly. Then he asks why I have such a big bandage on my head, and I tell him it's none of his business. Then he finally shuts up.

I have never been on a trip in a car before. Except in an ambulance or with Dr. Zuleger, I have only ridden in a car one single time. That was during the Easter vacation, when Uncle Sam Silver came by in his jeep. But we couldn't go on a trip in it; he only did a little circuit with me, up to the ruined church and back to Aunt Lou again.

Too bad Rena couldn't come. I asked Fräulein Urban, but she said no. I even offered to give up the promised ice cream. But Fräulein Urban said that Rena never took part in the collecting, so it would be unfair to all the others who had tried so hard, and I must appreciate that.

She's right. But all the same . . .

Rena really did wash my red blouse last night and she ironed it dry this morning before breakfast. I stood beside her and watched her.

"You're going to have ice cream and eat in a restaurant," she said. "Have you ever been in a restaurant before?"

No, of course I haven't. Except once: that was when the Welfare lady took me to the Hildegardis Children's Home. But that time I was so afraid that I didn't really notice anything. I've been in bars more often. In the Paradise, for instance. But I didn't tell Rena that, because I didn't want to think about it. And certainly not talk about it. People only go to restaurants to eat, that I know; I've already read about that. The man who brings in the food wears a tuxedo—I don't know what that looks like—and is called the waiter.

We drive past the railroad station, then through the bombed-out district, where only three or four buildings are still standing, and finally through the new suburbs. Now we are on the highway. Outside, fields and meadows are whizzing past us, women digging potatoes, a farmer with a wagon and an ox hitched to the front of it. I didn't know that it's so beautiful when you get out into the country. Or I forgot. Somehow I must have known it, of course, for when I was with Frau Kowalksi, I lived in the country. But she never let me out; I was only allowed to look out the window. I simply must talk to Rena about it and ask her if she's familiar with the countryside. Where did she live before? I have no idea, but I think in a city. Almost all of us came from cities.

Frau Lehmann drives much faster than Dr. Zuleger. The landscape goes by so fast that I can hardly keep up with it. My mind grows completely empty of thoughts and fills with pictures. I look and look and become very calm. I could keep on driving and looking that way forever. Through fields, meadows, forests, and every now and then a village.

But then we are there. Frau Lehmann parks the car in a space in front of a big, high wrought-iron gate. You have to buy a ticket if you want to go into the park. Frau Lehmann pulls out her wallet and Wolfi begins to whine that he wants some ice cream now. Why ever did they bring him? Fräulein Urban is carrying a shopping bag with sandwiches and a thermos of tea for us for lunch. "Because we aren't going to have dinner until evening—that's much nicer than dinner at noon," Fräulein Urban says.

The castle is gigantic. In the center there is a gate into the park, which begins right behind it. The park is so big that you can't see where it ends. There are curving gravel paths between closely mowed lawns that are encircled by flower beds, with fountains and pools in between them. Stone deer and dogs are lying in front of a huge fountain. And everywhere there are stone figures and vases standing on high pedestals. I have to stand still for a long time before I feel able to go on. Never have I seen anything like this. I had no idea that anything like this existed, something so beautiful, so vast.

Beside the broad main path with the flower beds and the fountains are pathways enclosed by straight, clipped hedges. Hedges like walls. We walk along the main path, turn into a hedged pathway, and suddenly we are among tall trees, as if we were in a forest. And new stone figures keep appearing.

Wolfi whines the entire time, but I don't pay any attention to him. As far as I'm concerned he can do whatever he wants, so long as he doesn't bother me. Not he, not his mother, not Fräulein Urban—I wish I were all by myself.

The paths between the tall trees are pleasantly shadowy. Suddenly a stone woman appears in front of me. She is standing on a pedestal in the middle of a little pond, as if she has just climbed out of the water. She is naked and carries a kind of hand towel over her shoulder. That's also made of stone, but the folds look as if they were made of fabric. The stone is smooth and white with gray shadings. The woman has her head bent slightly to the left. Her arms are white and round, her belly looks very soft. But the most beautiful things are her legs. She is standing on her left leg and has the right one slightly pushed forward, as if she were about to take a step. The light stone shimmers like skin. And the legs are formed so that you can clearly see the knees and the rounded calves. As if she were alive. And then the feet, with toes and toenails. But the most beautiful thing is her right knee.

She looks like a real woman. As if somewhere once a very beautiful woman climbed out of a pond and was walking through this splendid park and some magician was so taken with her that he wanted to keep her. "You shall never grow old," he said. "You shall remain as you now are, now at this moment." And then he turned her to stone. It didn't hurt her; she kept smiling, a stony smile now; she was turned to stone in the middle of a gesture. Even the stone is beautiful because she was so beautiful. Could she now be even more beautiful than she was in reality? Or perhaps the magician only dreamed her, and she is the way he imagined beauty to himself. A dream turned to stone.

Suddenly someone is putting an arm around my

shoulder. Fräulein Urban. "Why are you crying, Halinka?" she asks.

I haven't even noticed that I'm crying. "She is so beautiful," I say. "Her leg . . ." I don't know what to say. You can't describe something like that. And besides, she only needs to open her eyes and see for herself.

Fräulein Urban pulls me a little closer. "Come," she says, "we're going to eat. And then you'll get your ice cream."

I let her pull me toward a bench where Frau Lehmann and Wolfi are sitting and looking our way. I'm not hungry, and I don't even care about ice cream.

"You like it, don't you?" Frau Lehmann asks. "Now you're glad we came here, aren't you?"

Her singsong way of speaking suddenly isn't funny anymore. She fits right into this park.

"What are these stone figures called?" I ask, as I unwrap my sandwich. It's sliced cheese, which is also something special.

"Statues," Fräulein Urban says. "They are about two to three hundred years old."

I eat the cheese sandwich, drink tea out of a tin cup that Fräulein Urban has pulled out of her shopping bag, and look over at the trees behind which my statue has been standing for more than two hundred years. I have the feeling that she has been waiting for me. For me alone. And when I go away, she will be waiting for me to come back.

We have to leave the park to get the ice cream.

"I don't want to," I say. "I don't need any ice cream. I'd rather stay here."

Frau Lehmann and Fräulein Urban promise me that we will come right back. I don't want to go, but stupid Wolfi whines, and I have no choice but to follow the others. At the entrance Frau Lehmann arranges with the man at the gate for us to come back in on the same tickets. He promises we can, and we go along a few streets, of which I take little notice because my thoughts are still in the park, with the statues, especially with mine, the one that has waited for me for two hundred years. . . .

Suddenly we're standing in front of an ice-cream stand. Wolfi is an old hand at this; he wants a large waffle cone with raspberry and chocolate ice cream. I don't care what I have.

"Just look at the board and see all the flavors there are," Frau Lehmann says.

She sounds disappointed. She must have assumed that I would be utterly wild about ice cream. And normally I

would be too. It's not her fault that I can't get the statues out of my head. I consider the ice-cream flavors. "Banana," I say quickly. "Banana and chocolate."

Frau Lehmann smiles, satisfied. I also get a large waffle
cone. Frau Lehmann and Fräulein Urban only order
small cones with one scoop for themselves. We walk
back, licking our cones.

"Can I walk around alone for a little while?" I ask
Fräulein Urban softly when we are back in the park.

At first she hesitates, then she says, "Very well, but
don't leave the paths. And then come back here to the
fountain, to the deer."

I promise and go on alone.

The park belonged to real people once. People who
lived in this castle and could simply walk around here
without having to buy tickets. They saw everything
every day. They must also have had children who ran
around on these paths. Maybe they played dodgeball on
the lawns. Or they played hide-and-seek behind the
pedestals of the statues. They sat on the stone deer, dug
their heels into their sides, and cried "Giddyap!" If you
lived with so much beauty around you every day, you
would have to become a different person, I think.

Even if you consider that a whole lot of servants lived
in this gigantic castle, everyone must have had several

rooms. We live seven to one room. And Aunt Lou in her tiny furnished room. It seems so strange to me. If a person always had so much space around her, she would certainly develop a different way of moving.

I've never considered before that other people live differently. I've never considered, either, that in addition to the countless things in the world that are merely useful, like a pot or a pair of scissors, there are also other things that can cast a spell over a person just because they are beautiful. And rare. Suddenly I realize that, compared with useful things, beauty is an extra. But all the same, you absolutely have to have it. Anyhow, *I* will always have to have it—this I know for certain at this moment. Realizing this makes me want to cry again. But at the same time I am glad that my statue will be here for me to see it.

Aunt Lou is wrong to say that a person can imagine anything if she only thinks about it right. I couldn't have imagined all this, because I simply didn't know anything about it. It's complicated, Aunt Lou. You can only imagine things that you know about.

I have, of course, often heard the words *castle park*, or read them, but I didn't know what they meant. I think I just thought of a green area like the one in front of the train station.

I run along the main path and down each side path. Just as I am looking at the three stone children playing with a billy goat, Wolfi comes running up to me. "I've been looking for you," he yells. "Come with me. Back there there's a picture painted on the wall in a house. The end of the world. It really looks as if you could see forever and ever. Fräulein Urban says it's perspective. Come on, I'll show it to you."

"I don't care about your picture," I say and turn away. What do I care about a picture painted on a wall? I walk quickly back along the path. Then I am standing in front of my statue again. She is the most beautiful of all, she has such beautiful legs, such beautiful knees. How could anyone make something like that out of stone?

All at once Fräulein Urban is standing next to me and she places a hand on my shoulder. "Halinka," she asks, "why did you open the collecting box? Did you take any money out of it?"

For a long moment my head grows very light and my legs begin to tremble. Then I get control of myself again. "No," I say. "I was just so curious and wanted to know how full the box was. And then the wires wouldn't fit together again."

Her hand presses my shoulder somewhat more firmly. "Good," she says, "we'll say no more about it. We have to leave in a few minutes. We're going to go to the restaurant now."

She turns around. I look after her. I'm still a little wobbly, but that passes quickly. I think she knows, but I don't have to tell her if I don't want to. Perhaps I will tell her sometime and take dishwashing duty or kitchen duty or reception duty for punishment. Then afterwards I will really deserve this outing. For this is repayment for everything. Even the fear I suffered because of that lead seal and the wires. Everything is repaid, everything. God takes His time, but He repays with interest, Aunt Lou, you're right. Somehow a person is paid back for everything.

The little pond keeps me from touching my statue. Too bad. But perhaps it's just as well. No one ought to touch her. She is absorbed, she belongs only to herself. The stone looks cool, smooth, and beautiful. "Goodbye," I whisper to her. "I'll come again. I promise I'll come again someday."

I look up at her face. She has been standing there for more than two hundred years. Her head is raised against the blue sky. The birds have begun to sing in the shrubs and the trees; it's evening. I feel very small and at the same time large, very large. I think that's happiness. Or at least something like it.

Then I go back to the others.

We drive out of Schwetzingen in the car. In a village, Frau Lehmann stops in front of a restaurant. "The Green Oak," it says on a big sign. "Hotel and Dining Room."

There are at least twenty tables in the room, but it looks very different from our own dining room. There are dark draperies at the windows, and the tables are covered with white cloths. People are sitting at some of them. A waiter brings us the menu. He is wearing a black suit. Frankly, I imagined a tuxedo differently.

I know exactly what I want to eat; I don't need a menu. "A smoked pork chop," I say. "Please, could I have a smoked pork chop?"

"How nice, child," Frau Lehmann says. She appears to be really happy when I express a desire. Perhaps because her son, Wolfi, isn't satisfied with anything. He is a real fusspot. He insists on pancakes with applesauce.

"It's not on the menu, of course," the waiter says, "but I'm sure we can make it."

Wolfi is finally satisfied.

Fräulein Urban orders a glass of red wine with her meal, but it comes well before her food, so she has to order another. I watch her mistrustfully. What will happen if she gets drunk now? Will she start to scream and hit? But she doesn't order a third glass, and the wine just makes her cheerful. Frau Lehmann has mineral water, and Wolfi and I get apple juice. It's sweet and actually tastes like apples.

Finally the food comes. Now I really am hungry. The waiter puts a plate in front of me on which lies the smoked pork chop. It's pink with a whitish layer of fat between the meat and the bone. The bone is gray and porous at the place where it has been sawed through, like an old rubber ball, while the long, curved part looks as if it is covered with a silvery skin. And the entire chop is just as big and thick as I always imagined it. There are mashed potatoes and sauerkraut with it.

I watch Frau Lehmann and Fräulein Urban, who are eating their meat with knife and fork. They hold the knife in the right hand and the fork in the left. It looks easy when they do it, but when I try it myself it isn't so simple. But I manage. I cut little pieces off the pork chop and chew them very slowly so that nothing will escape me. It tastes strangely salty but very good. Never, it seems to me, have I ever eaten anything so good. I hardly remember the taste of that other smoked pork chop, that time on the trip from the sanatorium to the Hildegardis Children's Home. But that isn't important anymore, either, now that I know once more how smoked pork chop tastes. Good, very good. I certainly won't forget this taste ever again.

Frau Lehmann and Fräulein Urban often look over at me. Usually I don't like it when someone looks at me, but this time I don't care. When at the end I pick up the bone to chew on it, they laugh. I laugh too. For dessert there is even pudding, chocolate pudding, with many little blobs of whipped cream around the edge.

On the way home I close my eyes. It's almost dark outside anyway. Besides, I want to remember everything about this day. Really everything, so that I will never forget it. Especially my beautiful lady turned to stone.

When the car stops in front of the home, I am surprised at how fast the trip has gone. We get out. Frau Lehmann also gets out. She hugs me and kisses my hair. "I'm glad that you were the one who won the prize, Halinka," she says. "It was lovely being with you."

I feel like crying. But I don't. "Thank you, Frau Lehmann," I say. "It was a very nice trip. Many thanks." I don't even have to force myself to say thank you.

Fräulein Urban and I go up the steps together. It's already after lights-out. "Be quiet," she says to me softly. "You don't have to wake up the others. Sleep well, child."

"You too," I say. "And thank you."

She passes her hand over my hair. Then she goes to her apartment and I to our room.

Rena is still awake. I expected that. But I don't want to go to the luggage storeroom tonight. I only want to lie in bed and think of the statue. Or of beauty. I don't know. Anyhow, I have to be alone tonight.

We go into the washroom and stand next to each other, each at a washbasin, holding our hands under the cold water. "Don't be angry with me," I say to Rena. "Tomorrow I'll tell you everything. Tonight I can't. I have to think about it for a while first."

Rena is disappointed, I can see it. But of course she doesn't press me to tell. She would never do that. "Good," she says. "Tomorrow, then."

We go back to the room. She gives me a kiss.

I lie in bed, with my little doll in my hand under the covers, and go through the whole trip once more. Once, twice, three times. Rena doesn't cry. I don't know if she's asleep. But that isn't important at the moment. Tomorrow I will tell her everything, even about the lady of stone.

I close my eyes.

The park is so big that you can't see where it ends. There are curving gravel paths between closely mowed lawns that are encircled by flower beds, with fountains and pools in between them. Stone deer and dogs are lying in front of a huge fountain. And everywhere there are stone figures and vases standing on high pedestals. I have to stand still for a long time before I feel able to go on. Never have I seen anything like this. I had no idea that anything like this existed, something so beautiful, so vast. . . .

who
needs honey
when sugar
is just
as sweet?

I am in a strange home, where I don't know anyone. It is huge, with long corridors, and flights of stairs going up and down, and endless numbers of doors.

I run along the corridors as if someone were behind me. But each time I turn around, the corridor is empty, there is only me. My steps echo, and the echo reverberates from the walls. It sounds eerie, and I run even faster. Then suddenly I hear a voice that screams, "You just wait until I catch you, and then you're going to get the surprise of your life!" I'm sure I know the voice and frantically try to figure out who it belongs to, but I can't think. I only know that I have to get away, urgently.

Terrified, I tear open the next door and am standing in a room that looks entirely different from what I expected. Very different from our room. There are no beds in it, no simple wardrobe cupboards, no desks for doing homework.

It is a small room with brownish wallpaper. At the windows hang white net curtains and over them heavy, dark-green draperies that reach to the floor. In front of the window is a round table with a green tablecloth of velvet and four chairs around it. To the right, in the corner, I see a wooden bed, and on the bed lie a thick, puffy coverlet and a fat pillow with a crease in the middle. Just by the door there is an old-fashioned wardrobe chest with turned feet. The most striking thing, though, is a dresser on the left wall, an antique dresser decorated with a carving.

I know this room, I know it from somewhere. Perhaps I've dreamed it before. There isn't anyone in the room. It smells like . . . I have to think for a long time before it comes to me what it smells like. Like lilacs. And immediately I know that I haven't smelled lilacs in a long time. When was the last time? I don't know. I've forgotten.

Hesitantly I go over to the dresser and pull out one of the drawers. There is jewelry inside. I take out a necklace and look at it for a long time. It seems familiar to me somehow, as if I've seen it before. It's made of silver, dark, almost black, and has a strangely shaped pendant, a star with a green stone in the middle. Tears come to my eyes, but I'm not sad, I'm glad. I quickly open the next drawer, and more, and more, until all the drawers are open. All kinds of crazy things are in the drawers— jewelry, porcelain figures, bottles and little boxes, colored fabrics.

I pick up a piece of blue velvet and hold it against my face. How soft it is. Suddenly the door flies open and someone grabs me by the shoulder. Frightened, I jump and turn around.

It's Susanne. She's shaking me.

I quickly close my eyes again. I don't want to wake up, I want to keep on dreaming. What happens in that room? Who does the dresser with the jewelry belong to?

"Come on, get up!" She has room duty this week and is responsible for us all being ready on time. I get up and go to the washroom. When I come back, Rena has already made my bed. The gong rings, and we go down to the dining room together.

At breakfast Duro asks me how the trip was. I don't feel like talking. I'm still thinking about my dream.

So I just say, "Beautiful. It was very beautiful."

"Come on, tell," Inge says. "Don't make us drag it out of you."

I look sideways, and Rena nods slightly. "We're just curious," she says, encouraging me. "You can understand that."

I begin to tell. But not about the park, about the restaurant. How the room looked, what the waiter was wearing, how the tables were covered, and what we ate. I tell and tell and don't know for sure anymore whether it's all true, what I'm saying, whether it really was so. But it doesn't matter. So then I also describe the dresser with the carving that suddenly is also there in the restaurant, and I tell them about a woman who was wearing a very beautiful silver necklace with a star-shaped pendant in whose center was a green stone. They listen to me, spellbound.

That's all right with me. They should be content and not ask me about the park. That belongs only to me. The others wouldn't understand it anyway. I don't even know how to explain what I experienced there.

But then Duro asks me, "And how was the park?"

I put on an indifferent face. "The way parks always are," I say, as if I've seen hundreds of castle parks already. "Lawns, flower beds, paths, benches."

Imperceptibly, Rena moves her hand a little to the right so that it touches mine.

I can breathe easily again. "Now, will you quit questioning my head off? I just told you it was beautiful."

Rena stands up. She has table duty and gathers up the dishes to take them to the kitchen. I help her. I would prefer not to go to school today. I could, of course, say that I don't feel well. No, Fräulein Urban wouldn't believe me. And besides, I really don't want to lie to her. Not today. So I go down to our classroom with Rena.

I don't take in much of the lesson at all—my mind is somewhere else. I keep seeing the statue in front of me, with a silver necklace. Or the statue in the little room with the green curtains. She looks entirely different there. And in between I hear Aunt Lou's voice. "Learn, Halinka. You must learn as much as you can. What you have learned, no one can ever take away from you."

Tomorrow, Aunt Lou, tomorrow I'll pay attention again, I promise. How exactly do you say "beautiful" in Polish? Oh yes, *piękny. Ta kobieta piękna*—what a beautiful woman.

Before dinner, when the mail is handed out, Fräulein Urban hands me a letter, a letter from Aunt Lou. I shove it into my skirt pocket and sit down at the table.

Rena has seen me. "I'm going to write a letter to my mother this afternoon," she whispers to me. "I tried yesterday, but it didn't come out right. But surely today . . ." She reaches for her fork.

When I'm sitting on the toilet after dinner and open the letter, a ten-mark note falls out and flutters to the floor. I quickly pick it up.

Travel money. Aunt Lou wants me to come. She misses me. In her letter she says that she is looking forward to seeing me.

But there is some other news in it. Next week Uncle Sam Silver is going back to the United States. He has been transferred to another unit. No word of marriage. So that's that, Aunt Lou. I got my hopes up too soon. I will have to wait here longer until you find a husband.

Too bad. I liked Uncle Sam Silver. Perhaps I would like any man that Aunt Lou loved. Yet he has to be right for her. Of course some women fall in love with the wrong men, I know that, too. But not Aunt Lou, of that I am sure. It will happen, sometime, somehow. "I am very sad," Aunt Lou has written, "and Uncle Sam Silver is, too. But that's the way it is with soldiers. You can never know how long they will stay anywhere."

Ten marks. I have double travel money. I don't need to use any of the other money, I don't have to find an excuse. Somehow everything has arranged itself all on its own.

Just before the end of the midday rest I go to Fräulein Urban.

"I would like to go to see my aunt on Saturday," I say.

"Did you get a letter from her?" she asks.

I shake my head. I have, of course, gotten a letter, but I don't want to show it to her. Uncle Sam Silver is none of her business, only Aunt Lou's and mine.

"You know that my aunt can't write German properly," I say.

Fräulein Urban frowns. "I've already told you many times that she must write something if she wants you to come for the weekend. Or at least call. You know perfectly well that I can't just let you go. Can she be reached by telephone?"

"Yes," I say. "Now is the best time. She has just gotten to work."

I write the telephone number on a piece of paper, and Fräulein Urban goes to her telephone, which is standing on a little table with high, curving legs. She places the call and holds the receiver out to me.

A strange woman is on the phone. I say that I would like to speak with Aunt Lou. The woman is grouchy, she grumbles, she'll have to go look for Aunt Lou. The boss won't be pleased if these personal calls keep coming during working hours.

I wait patiently until finally I hear Aunt Lou's voice. At first I can't get a word out because suddenly I am so hot. Then I explain to her that she must first say in writing or by telephone that I am allowed to come to her for the weekend.

"What's all this about?" she asks. "I sent you money, isn't that clear enough?"

"All the same," I say, and suddenly I think of two things: the ten marks behind the beam, and Aunt Lou's sofa. It's quite narrow, of course, but fortunately Rena and I are not very fat.

"Aunt Lou," I ask, "can I bring a friend?"

She's quiet for a moment.

"Please, Aunt Lou," I say quickly. "You will love her. Love with an *o* and an *e*."

And then Aunt Lou says, "*Meshuggener kop!* Silly one! Love is an important word. I know perfectly well that you spell it with an *o* and an *e*. Of course you can bring your friend.

"And now put on Fräulein Urban," she says.

"Thank you, Aunt Lou." I can't get the words out fast enough because my throat is tickling. "Thank you, and I'll see you Saturday. We'll be on the train that leaves here at 2:27. Oh, Aunt Lou, I'm so looking forward to it."

I hold the receiver out to Fräulein Urban. I can't hear

everything Aunt Lou is saying, and she goes on for quite a long time. Fräulein Urban listens, and then she laughs too. When Aunt Lou laughs, everyone has to laugh with her.

When Fräulein Urban finally hangs up, she says, "It's all right, you can go. And you can take a friend. Shall I guess who she is, this friend?"

"Rena," I say. "Renata, who else?"

She strokes my head as I open the door. Like yesterday. "When do you have to go to Dr. Zuleger again?"

"Tomorrow. He's going to take the stitches out."

She strokes my head once more, and I leave.

Rena will be amazed. I have to laugh when I imagine her face. Slowly I walk along the corridor to the washroom. It's kind of a custom with me. When for some reason I don't want to go back to the room right away, I hold my hands under the water in the washroom. It doesn't matter what the reason for it is. It always calms me.

The water is pleasantly cool. I bend and drink a few swallows and wet my face. My face looks back at me from the mirror. Suddenly I have the feeling I look different, older. I lift the bandage and stare at my wound. It's healing well, Dr. Zuleger said. No one will see the scar if I let my hair grow over it. Tomorrow, when the stitches are out, I certainly won't need such a big bandage.

It occurs to me that I have just opened the door to good fortune.

I dry my face and leave the washroom.

In front of the door to our room I stop. I'm going to tell Rena right now. I put my hand in my skirt pocket. There is my doll. She's five and a quarter inches long; I measured her. She's just like me; I'm not very big, either. Rena painted her celluloid hair black again.

Aunt Lou, dear Aunt Lou, who needs honey when sugar is just as sweet?